MY LITTLE DIAMOND

Brooke Oatley

Contents

I n everyone's life, there is always a moment that changes every-thing drastically. Maybe you meet the love of your life. Maybe you lose someone dear. Or you have the worst accident that changes everything.

For Mark Drummond, a officer for the Chicago police department, that was the day he was shot. 6 years in the force, nothing prepares you for what happens on the day you are injured in the line of duty. Or worse. Mark not only was shot, he lost his leg and a large chunk in his arm. On top of it all, engaged to be married, fiance of 4 years, leaves him when he needs her the most.

Despite being as strong as he is, Mark is alone, in the worst pain, and struggling to accommodate his new life. Everything seemed hopeless until he started physical therapy and meets the perky occu-pational therapist, Anya Jones. She brings a smile to everyone in a room. Not only smiles, but she starts stirring deep emotions in the dying heart inside Mark's chest. The longer he spends with her, the more he finds out how similar they actually are.

Double Shot

Heavy boots stormed the back alley in Chicago as Mark pursued the heartless son of a bitch who just robbed and killed an innocent old woman over her pocket-book. It was a horrible sight to behold. Mark and a few other officers were on their lunch break at the local food truck when they heard the shrill screams of the poor woman trying to fight off the bastard that was threatening her with a knife. Everything happened so fast that she was on the ground before anyone realized what was going on. Mark saw red as a puddle spilled over the sidewalk. The group of officers darted across the road to chase him. Blood boiling, heart racing, and sweat dripping from his face from the summer heat, he got closer and closer. The other officers were not far behind, but Mark was faster. Despite being more of an IT guy in the department, he took care of himself and worked out daily. The scruffy, unkempt murderer darted to the left in a poor effort to lose him. Not a smart move on his part. Like the typical criminals in the city, he had a good layout of the alleys. Dead end. He was cornered. Mark hollered at the man to drop. The man turned and he saw the man's face .The perpetrator's face twitched, eyes pin-points, and his arms shook. A terrified look on his face, realizing what he had done. He robbed and killed that old woman for money to get another hit. Mark growled low, pure rage engulfed him. That poor innocent woman. Someone's mother, grandmother, friend. Gone.

"Get on the ground! NOW!" Mark warned, going to withdraw his gun. Not fast enough. Mark cursed as he saw the murderer draw a hidden weapon. Bang! Bang!

Nothing in this life prepares a person for the day they are shot. An annoying ringing filled Marks ears as he stared at the man in front of him with a gun pointed, arm shaking violently. His eyes were widened. Terrified, but not totally there. First murder, then shooting a cop. Probably suffering effects of withdrawal or being high. Everything was happening too fast for Mark to register, that the man probably had no clue what planet he was on.

Mark's eyes looked down as he felt a hot wetness pooling over his thigh. How he was still standing was nothing short of amazing. His adrenaline already pulsing full force was making the blood pump out of his artery faster. Another gun metal shot and Mark went down, not having much time to react he pulled the trigger on his own pistol, downing the man as he went to his knees. Pain sieged through his right arm. Mark let out a blood curdling bellow to alert his fellow officers. Vision spotting, Mark collapsed on the gravel scattered alley way, panting and writhing in pain. The last thing he saw were the other officers approaching and yelling. Mark couldn't hear any of it before darkness engulfed him.

(First update! Unedited, just wanted to give a sneak peak and show I am still alive!)

Here is Mark Drummound :3 *I LOVE Micheal Stokes photography! This gentleman really captures how I imagined Mark* ~Enjoy the eye candy!

Losing a Part of You

S irens blared, people shouted, but the darkness still remained. White hot pain was the only thing Mark felt. Pain and a part of him fading.

'We have to take the leg.' a muffled voice stated flatly, a pang of regret laced the words.

'What? Leg? Take?' Hazy thoughts slowly started to turn. Struggling to open his eyes for even a second, Mark was able to see he was in a hospital. The hustle and bustle of the beeping and metal sounds began to take over as his consciousness started to return. 'No...don't take my leg...'

"Get him to the OR NOW! NURSE!" A loud voice threw orders like a dictator.

Mark's body felt paralyzed, it took every ounce of strength he didn't have to turn his head. Things started to become clearer. Tubes of IVs, more figures than he could make out of the nurses and doctors, and the blood...his blood...and packages of donor blood hanging. Mark remembered everything up until when he got shot. Nothing about the others finding him, or getting him to a hospital. Mark's hazy gaze traveled over his body, down to gushes of blood coming from his leg. "No..." he croaked. His throat scratched and felt like someone shoved cotton in his mouth. He was so dry. 'Please not my leg...." but the words only remained in his mind, he couldn't speak anything else.

"Sedate him!" The doctor ordered, taking notice to his regaining consciousness.

Good thing, Mark tried to move and the pain was even worse than when the bullet bit him. He let out a gurgled groan and tensed up, causing a heart monitor to spike.

A stern looking nurse pulled back on a syringe in a small vial before inserting it into the IV site, making Mark's mind go fuzzy again. The darkness returned.

Two days later...

Mark shifted in the uncomfortable hospital bed, glancing out the window. Exhaustion and anger plastered his handsome face. The last two days had been Hell. He had just been moved from the ICU to a normal recovery room, and for that he was grateful. Now he could see Lori, his fiance. He needed her right now, to have someone to hold.

His eyes glanced down to where his legs...leg laid beneath the white thin cloth the hospital called blankets. Biting his lip for what seemed like the hundredth time he replayed what the surgeon told him once he came to.

'Mr. Drummound...the damage to your right lower leg was too severe for us to save...and with the amount of blood loss...we had to amputate below the knee. We were, however, able to save your arm. It will leave a nasty scar.' The doctor explained while examining the wound dressings. 'Once everything heals, we will be able to start you on physical therapy and fitted for a prosthetic.'

He had tried to sound hopeful for Mark, but seeing the look on his face made him shut up real quick. Things would never return to 'normal' for Mark now. He would just have to adjust. Right now, he just wanted Lori. She had to be worried sick, especially being unable to talk to him the last couple days. Mark was constantly fading in and out of consciousness thanks to the morphine the nurse kept pushing into him. He was grateful to sleep through most of it. Now that he was in a normal room he had a PCA to control it himself. Of course, he was maxed out. Having a limb cut off had to be the worst pain anyone could imagine. The pain signals made him still feel like the bullet was ripping through him over and over...except not. Fucking phantom pain. Mark rarely cried, but this was enough to bring any man to tears. His arm hurt too, but he was able to ignore it. Closing his eyes he rested his head against the flat rectangles being passed off as pillows. Everything under the sun ran through his head. Would he recover in time for the wedding? How would he work? There was no way he could go back into the field. He could continue IT work at the department, but it wasn't the same as getting out there on the streets. What about when they had kids? Could he still be able to run after them?

A million more thoughts raced until there was a knock on his door. Mark's eyes snapped open and he realized he was falling asleep again. Damn morphine. His head spun slightly and he fought back a wave of nausea. Reaching for his water and taking a small sip he looked at the doorway.

Lori.

(edited)

Cold Hearted

Lori. Her jet black hair was flat ironed to her shoulders and her brown eyes were dusted perfectly with her favorite purple eyeshadow. The woman was never out of place in her looks. A little high maintenance but she was a business woman and never faltered in the man driven world of law. They had met when Lori was running a case that Mark had been the arresting officer. Love at first sight. She was everything he looked for in a woman. Strong, independent, and dynamite in bed. She had been very subtle with her flirting and their first date had led them back to his place. A war for dominance was pure fire. Mark loved it.

"Lori, baby..." Mark said with a sigh of relief. But something clouded her brown eyes and her face was flat. "You have no idea..." he breathed, "how badly I needed to see you..." This was a weak moment for him. He was lost, he was depressed. Mark held his arms out to her to encourage her to come to him. Her warmth was the only thing he needed right now to feel somewhat whole again.

She hesitated a moment; something Lori never did. Grinding her teeth she finally spoke after what seemed like an eternity, but she didn't move from her spot in the doorway. "Is it true? Did they take your leg...?" There was little emotion in her voice. Her eyes went from the bandaging on his arm to the form of the blankets where his legs were. The cloudiness came back in her eyes as she took notice.

Mark's brows furrowed and his arms dropped back to his side. Didn't the doctor talk to her? A sharp pang naggled in his chest. Something was off. Glancing down, Mark nodded. "From my knee down..." pausing he looked back up at her, "The bullet splintered and severed most of the muscle and the artery. They said there was no other option..." Why wasn't she coming to him? Perhaps she was just in disbelief as much as he was. They never really faced anything trying like this before, so he didn't really know what she was like if she was worried. Lori never worried. She was too confident. This had to be her worry. He gave a crooked smile, "I'm okay, baby. It could have been worse. I could be dead." He laughed bitterly. "We might have to postpone the wedding a couple months but-"

"I can't marry you." Lori said without batting an eyelash.

It was that moment, if it had a sound effect it would have been the sound of a car crash. A big one. "What?" Mark uttered in pure, visible confusion.

She stood there in the doorway, steel backbone. "I cannot be married to half a man. To have people look at us with such...pity..." She showed no remorse, like he was someone she was persecuting in the courtroom. Adjusting her purse she took a step forward. "It's hard enough being a woman in my field. I cannot look weak. Especially taking the partnership in New York. You would not be healed by the time the move comes."

Cue more car crashes. "You're kidding, right?" Mark gave a disbelief laugh. What the Hell kind of joke was this?! "Lori...now is not the time for jokes like this...I just lost my fucking leg. I could have died!" Mark growled. A deep part of him knew this wasn't a joke. Lori didn't joke. "What the fuck, Lori?"

Still no change in her emotion as she stepped closer to him, removing her engagement ring. "Don't worry, I will call everything off and take care of cancelling the reservations. It will cost to cancel this late, but I will take care of it." No one could be this heartless. No one. Or so he thought. 6 years in the force, Mark saw a lot of heartless shit, but the last 3 days had shown him a whole new level of cruelty. "Your parents are also on their way. I told them what happened."

"LORI!" Mark threw the blankets off and made a failed attempt to try and get up, almost forgetting the most important thing. Monitors went haywire and a second wave of nausea swept over him "You're leaving me?!" He yelled, "I love you! What kind of heartless bitch just leaves someone after an accident?! What happened to the vows we were going to take?! What the fuck would you have done if this happened after the wedding?!" His heart rate increased as he screamed at her.

"This was an unanticipated obstacle, an error on my part, given your dangerous field." She stated in a matter-of-fact tone. Her voice never raised, but cut through a room like it was a blade. Taking a single step closer, she handed him her engagement ring. A carat and a half pure diamond with two slightly smaller accent stones. It had cost Mark a fortune, but he would have given her the moon on a ring if he could have. She was his everything. Or so he thought. Sure she was rough around the edges, but Mark thought he saw something in her that was different. Looks like he was wrong. "I'm sure you will find someone else who won't mind." She said in the softest voice she could muster...which wasn't much.

The ring laid in Mark's hand and he stared down at it as she took a long look at him. He sat there, in a hospital gown, 5 o'clock shadow dusted his normally clean shaven face. His hair was oily from not having a proper shower and now the bandages around his arm and his stump were beginning to redden. "Lori...I love you..." he whispered.

She said nothing.

Did she even love him back? Or did she just say it to him as a habit or a response.

Mark looked up at her, confused. Seeing her in a new light. "Did you even love me back?"

Still she remained silent, almost like she couldn't respond to him. For the first time since he met her, she was speechless.

"LORI!" Mark raised his voice.

Half a Man?

"L ORI!" Mark raised his voice. This situation was backwards. Normally it was the man who was the one breaking things off and the woman begging. He hated this weak feeling, but dammit he was human. He loved her. 4 years of his life were now gone. They had planned a life. They had discussed moving to New York for Lori to become a partner in a large firm once the wedding was over. Mark had even looked into the NYPD. Kids...Mark wanted a big family like he had. Lori had been an only child, and while she didn't seem the mothering sort, she had been open to having a child. Everything they had planned. Poof. Gone. Just like that.

"You were a good match. But things have changed. I am truly sorry it had to come to this. I will be leaving." She turned to leave. "You may keep the condo, I won't be needing it after I go to New York. I will have my things out before your discharge." she tossed over her shoulder as if she was being a very generous person. "I wish you the best in life, Mark."

"LORRIII!!!" Mark yelled, trying to stand and immediately regretting the forgetful choice as he met the floor. Every alarm in his room sounded off and several nurses came running in. Where had they been when the machines first started going off as his heart rate increased? Scrambling around they hoisted him back up onto the bed, questioning him with several things at one time, mostly asking if he was ok. His mind was blank as he watched Lori walking away without a second glance. The nurses looked as well, one picking up the ring and handing it to him, saying nothing. They had heard everything. That explained why they didn't go in. Concern and apologetic looks showed on each of them.

The nurses began to redress Mark's bloody bandages, a senior nurse giving him the business about overdoing it and causing his wound to get worse if he wasn't more careful. Mark only heard parts of her nagging. He didn't even feel the throbbing pain in his leg. He was numb. It didn't take them long to finish, leaving him alone in his room and his head.

How could she have done something like this? Half a man? How did this make him any less of one? Plenty of people lived normal lives with missing limbs. Hell some even went on to be track racers or body builders; healthy, exciting people. But what were things going to be like? He would go home to an empty house...full of memories of her. Everyone he knew would look at him with pity. That is the last thing he wanted.

Mark's dark thoughts were interrupted by a gasp and cry. Turning his head, the blur of his mother came into view and snatched him into her tiny frame before he knew what had happened. "MY BABY!"

She shrieked, sobbing uncontrollably. His dad entered shortly after talking to one of the nurses about his condition.

Yup...this was not what he wanted either.

The next was 20 minutes almost as bad as getting shot...having to explain everything that had transpired to his parents.

"That bitch!" Diane shot like an arrow after hearing what had happened. "How could she just up and leave you!" She wanted to leave this hospital and track down Lori and show her a thing or two. She had never liked the woman from the start. Something about her just rubbed her the wrong way. Honestly, she was a little happy that she was gone. Just not at the way she had done it.

"Calm down." Mark's father, Ray, shook his head, arms folded over his meaty chest. But there was no stopping his wife once she got started. The woman was 5'1 and Hell on wheels. A total mama bear when it came to her cubs.

Typically, Mark would have been thrilled to see them. He and his parents were very close. As well as his 2 older brothers and younger sister. Right now he wanted nothing more than to be alone. That wasn't happening any time soon. Mark looked outside the door at his younger sister, Maria, trembling scared like a lost puppy.

"Minnie..." Because she was obsessed with Disney from the time she was a baby and Minnie Mouse had been her favorite, Mark always called her Minnie. His eyes softened when he saw her teary eyes. She was the tender age of 8. Having a large gap between their ages didn't stop them from being close. He and his older brothers, Philip and

Evan ,were very protective of her. "Hey hey...don't cry. Big bro is okay." Mark tried to give her a goofy smile.

"Did you die?!" She ran to him and hugged him tightly.

"Nah, kiddo. I'm too strong for that." Mark ruffled her chocolate curls and pulled her into a tight hug, ignoring the shooting pain in his arm as he did so. Stay strong for Minnie. She was the one person he could never show weakness around. Not his baby sister. He was her hero. Holding her tight in his arms as she sobbed away, Mark glanced up at his parents who remained silent.

"Where's Aunt Lori?" She sniffled as she pulled away, strands of her curls sticking to her cheeks, snot running down her nose.

Things just wouldn't stop. Mark signed and looked up, gritting his teeth. "Maria."

Maria blinked, Mark only used her given name when he was being very serious.

"Lori and I broke up. She wanted to move to New York for a very important job." Mark hated to lie to her, but she was so young. "I couldn't just leave my baby sister behind, now could I?" he smiled softly and kissed her forehead.

Maria stared at him for a moment "But...I was gonna be a flower girl."

So simple.

Mark shook his head, "I know, Minnie. You will one day, I promise." More lies...at least, that's what it felt like. Who would want him now? Lori had left so easily.

Maria shot a look over to their parents "He should marry that pretty lady we saw on the way in here!" She shifted back to look at Mark, her blue eyes bright and excited again. "She was so pretty! She had on those blue nurse clothes, and, and looong pretty blonde hair, like Aunt Rachel! And she had a bigggggg smile!" Maria made the biggest smile she could mimic. "Not like Lori! She never smiled!"

Mark gave a shaky laugh, "Minnie, it's going to be a long time before your big brother finds another girl...I have to get used to having 1 leg." he admitted.

Maria glanced down, she knew what had happened. Even being a kid she knew deep down that it would be hard on her older brother.

Diane gently removed her daughter from the bed, to keep her from hurting Mark further. "Evan and Phil are going to be helping you once you get out of the hospital."

Mark glanced away, "I don't think that will be anytime soon. The doctor said I need physical therapy as well as occupational therapy...I might have to go to a rehab." The thought of having to stay in a hospital setting any longer pissed him off further. Mark gave his parents a look when he noticed his sister wasn't paying attention. He wanted them to go.

Ray rubbed his neck. "You sure you will be okay?" he asked.

Mark just nodded, "I'm sorry. I'm just not feeling well. I know you came all the way here..."

Diane kissed his forehead and they said their goodbyes, once again leaving Mark to himself. Which was just what he wanted. To replay things over and over again until he felt himself sinking further into a pit of despair.

Late into the night, Mark groaned and shifted violently in his bed. Pain pulsated through his body and he woke up drenched in sweat. Shivering enough to make his teeth chatter, Mark wasn't sure if he was hot or freezing. His heart monitor was going violent. A bellow echoed through the room as it felt like a hot blade was being dug into Mark's leg, causing a swarm of nurses to sprint into his room shouting at each other and holding him down as he began to thrash. Mark had spiked a fever and started to seize.

Give into the Darkness

A few weeks passed by in a foggy blur and Mark remained in the ICU. He had become septic and his body went down quick. Luckily the hospital had one of the best sepsis teams in the state and were able to keep him alive. The first week and a half they had him on a respirator. Once he was finally awake, they were able to remove it and monitored him around the clock to be sure he was safe to breath on his own.

The day the aid came in to help him bath was a bit of a shock to him. In just those few short weeks, Mark had lost quite a bit of weight, making him feel weaker than before. Not only his body, but his mind. Mark couldn't help but give into the dark thoughts that had taken over. Wishing himself dead. What else was there to do except lay up in the bed and think. He wasn't much of a TV person before the accident, and didn't want to start. Never before in his life did he ever imagine being this low. For so long, he had never understood how people could ever get to that point until he was finally in it. He gave up. This was his rock bottom. It felt like no end in sight. He was broken; Mind, body and spirit. So much for thinking he would be a marathon runner like so many others after this.

Finally after another 2 weeks, Mark was moved to a rehab unit. His brothers came in to visit him once they got him moved. They wanted to encourage him to work hard to get out of the hospital, but were both horrifyingly shocked to see him a shell of his former self. His cheeks were sunken in, his eyes had dark bags under them, he had refused to shave, skin ashen. A permanent scowl marked his once handsome face. Just a few short weeks had done so much damage.

Evan looked at his brother, Phil, words not needed. Mark was asleep, thank God, because the look on their faces was full of shock and horror.

Phil pulled Evan to whisper to him, "What the fuck happened!? He looks like a Goddamn skeleton!" Phil was pissed, thinking that the hospital had mistreated his brother and were not taking care of him.

The two brothers began to vent to one another about the treatment of their brother. Thinking they were being quiet, but not so much. An older, heavy set nurse with frizzy silver hair, glasses, and a limp from a bad knee, came up to them. "He refuses to do anything." She said with concerned eyes and a huff. "We moved him here 3 days ago. He hardly eats...I offered to get him a shaving kit...Hell, one orderlie offered to bring him food from the restaurant down the street. Man just sits there staring off into space." Shaking her head she glanced into the room at him. "Word has it...when he arrived at the recovery unit after..." she trailed off, referring to his leg, "A woman came in and broke off their engagement...apparently the cunt called him half a man!" The old nurse got red in the face, obviously heated about the audacity of the bitch. Shaking her head she straightened herself, holding up a hand to excuse her outburst "The other nurses had unfortunately heard the whole ordeal...Then...that night, he had a seizure and went septic...recovered physically...for the most part." Her gaze softened to sadness, "But not his heart...none of the PTs can get him moving...He has given up." As if she needed to tell them, it was obvious.

Evan and Phil stared at her, unable to speak. Some relief washed over them to know the hospital was trying, but the concern remained that their brother had lost all his hope. The woman continued on. "I wish Anya were here...She picked a heck of a time to be off...I bet she would help him get in gear..." The nurse tapped her foot impatiently, "They won't let him stay here if he doesn't try." She warned. "Been here 25 years and never seen anything from someone so young...older folks, yes..."

Phil crossed his arms and raised a brow, "Who's Anya?" he questioned the nurse, glancing at her name tag that read Lisa.

"Only the best Physical therapist we have. That girl can get anyone and everyone on the track to living on their own." Lisa smiled proudly. "Studied under old Dr. Fillmore before he retired."

The two had no idea who she was talking about, but they also wished this mystery girl was around to get their brother in gear. Swallowing a lump in his throat, Evan turned and made his way in to see his younger brother.

As if he sensed their presence, Mark groaned and opened his eyes to see who was there, thinking it was one of the nurses coming in to assess him for the umtenth time that day. "Evan?" He questioned taking notice of the large figure standing in front of his bed with a slight scowl on his face. "Phil...what are you guys doing here?"

Phil ran a hand through his hair, "Mom was worried. Told us to come check in on ya." He could see the cloudiness cross his younger brother's eyes when the words came out. "What the Hell is going on Mark? You are just laying in this fucking bed wasting to nothing." Phil was the brother without a filter, he always spoke his mind. Tended to get himself into trouble from time to time with it, which was why he worked from home and avoided people most of the time.

Evan elbowed him in the stomach with a death glare to watch his mouth. Before he was able to retaliate, Mark spoke up.

"Fuck off." He growled. "What is the point anymore? Can't do shit now, my career is gone just like my Goddamn leg." Mark did spend a lot of time working IT for the police department, but he also spent a lot of time being active on the front. "My fiance left! Calling me half a fucking man. She is right. What kind of woman is going to want me now? Just up and left like I was just another business deal she didn't want part of because it wouldn't benefit her anymore." Everything bubbled up and exploded out of him, shocking both of his brothers. Mark was never one to explode like this, but when he did, he was a force to be reckoned with. The words continued to spill out of him, leaving Evan and Phil staring at him, allowing him to vent. "I can't run after Minnie anymore! I am not her strong big brother anymore!"

Mark felt hot tears stinging his eyes. It had been years since he cried. He felt like he was no longer his sister's hero like this. Fuck Lori, she was dead to him.

(I cannot imagine the pain and changes that comes with losing a limb...but I admire so many of them who still continue on and don't let it hold them back. Which is a huge reason I am writing this story. I have not seen many stories about amputees. I hope ya'll are enjoying the story thus far. And another thing: FUCK LORI, that cunt LOL I hated writing her character. What a cold hearted bitch!!)

Rejuvenated

S ucking in a deep breath of the fresh air that blew Anya's long hair side to side she stepped out of her car. It had been a nice time off, but Anya was ready to get back to the old grind. Management had pushed her into taking a vacation for once. So after a week and a half she was well rested and ready to get herself and others moving. Typically she hated being away for even the weekend, but a whole week felt like she was abandoning her patients. Even though most of them were also telling her to take a break. Reluctantly she took her week vacation and caught up on many chores she had been neglecting as well as visited her grandparents in New Mexico.

Making her way inside, Anya was greeted by many of her patients and coworkers who were sitting outside the rehab, enjoying the warming weather. "Glad to see you back, Anya! How was New Mexico?" One aide asked as he wheeled out a patient with a large cast over his leg.

Giving a short description of her visit she headed in where she was greeted by her favorite nurse, Lisa. Anya saw a look of relief wash over the older woman when she caught sight of her, "Oh thank God you are back!" Lisa exclaimed, walking as quick as her arthritic knee would take her. Anya blinked in confusion as Lisa continued on, trying to catch her breath. The woman needed to retire and take it easy, but like Anya, she just kept going. "I think we got your hardest patient yet..." Allowing her gaze to shift to the room where Mark currently resided in Lisa filled her in on the details.

At the end, Anya was on the verge of tears. How could someone be so cruel? She thought as she looked over at Mark again. She knew what it was like to be in his position physically, but she had the greatest support system she could have ever asked for. Not knowing what the future would hold for you was the hardest part about having an accident. Swallowing she thought back to her own accident.

It was her 18th birthday and she was on her way to her Aunt's house where they were holding her large celebration with all her friends and family. A drunk driver struck her car and sent her barreling over a guardrail and into a small wooded area. Her car had rolled several times according to the report and damage to her Jeep. Anya didn't remember any of it. The only thing she remembered was seeing the car whipping around a tractor trailer and hitting her going at least 80 in a 45 zone. She woke up in the hospital hooked up to a ventilator a month later. The accident had caused so much damage, the EMS and police officers on the scene were surprised she was even alive. Said her seat belt was the only reason for that, but when she went forward, large amount of glass and metal got behind her and caused many of the scars she now sported. As well as hot oil burns. Once she woke up she was so confused as to what had happened, but that all washed away when she tried to sit up once they removed the tube from her throat to allow her to breath on her own. She couldn't move or feel. The doctors told her she was paralyzed. Anya could still remember the words echoing inside of her that she would probably never walk again. The damage done to her vertebrae had severely impaired her in addition to the large number of scars across her back and neck. The few she had on the front half of her body were minor, which was a miracle. The surgeons discussed with her and her parents about going in for several surgeries to remove and repair the damage, but it came at a great cost. One wrong move and she would really never be able to move again and need to live on a ventilator for the rest of her life. The damage was great, but the outcome would possibly allow her mobility again.

Anya insisted they do the surgery as soon as possible. Her parents were both for and against it. Seeing their only daughter lying in a hospital bed. Her father cursed the man who had nearly killed her to Hell, wishing he could have gotten his hands on him. The man had hit three other cars and was pronounced dead on the scene. To Anya's relief, the others who had been struck walked away with minor injuries. One car had a couple who were on their way home from the hospital with their newborn baby.

Anya was determined to get out of the hospital bed. The surgery had taken numerous hours and several of the best surgeons in the state were working on her. The recovery was painful, but she was grateful for the slow return of her feeling. Though some days it became too much and morphine did not touch it. It felt as if someone had placed searing hot coals on her spinal cord. She would lay in bed those days and cry, she didn't want to be moved or sit in a wheelchair. It was a strong mental battle to get better and fight the depression...or let it take over and win. It wasn't until she tried doing physical therapy that she became the most discouraged. So many insisted she would never walk again, despite regaining the use of her arms and hands, even if it was only slight. Many had refused to take her as a client. It wasn't until she was moved to the rehab unit of Dr. Fillmore. He pushed Anya to her breaking point every single day. It took well over a year and a half, but his constant, and somewhat unorthodox approach to medicine combined with Anya's resilience, she was able to walk. Now at the age of 24, Anya was one of the hospital's top Physical therapists, and had taken over for Dr. Fillmore when he retired. It came to a surprise to so many, despite his advancing age, once he had completed Anya's therapy, he retired, having completed his hardest task in his lifetime. While she had been working on her therapy, she had started classes to get her degree. Knowing exactly what she wanted to do with her life. Inspire and help those whose shoes she had been in at one point. He trained her in his methods and she took to them quickly. Anya worked with those who were considered "lost causes" and she loved it. She loved helping people discover the strength they never knew was inside of them until she forced it out and got them going.

Anya shook her head, realizing she was staring at the man and Lisa was still talking to her. She got a good look at the man. He looked a fright, and from what Lisa was telling her, she had her work cut out for her. Straightening her scrubs she made her way over to his room to open the curtains and let in some sunlight. "Wakey wakey, eggs and bakey!" Anya chimed as she entered the room.

Mark groaned and rubbed his eyes, shooting a load of curses as he glared at the person who woke him. Stopping short when he saw Anya. He felt his heart almost stop and he was not entirely sure why. Her long golden hair reached down to her butt, then she turned to face him once the windows were open, he got a good look at her bright face. How the Hell could someone be so cheery in the morning? "What the Hell? Is that how you wake all your patients?"

"Yup!" Anya grinned as she closed the door to his room. "Alrighty, time to get you up and out of this bed before your ass gets a bedsore." She really had learned some unorthodox methods from Old Dr. Fillmore, and she knew when and who to apply them to.

Blinking, a little stunned he stared at the crazy, hyped up on coffee woman that was waltzing around his room. He also grimaced when he realized she was going to get him up. This was the first real attempt since he was moved. "And just how do you plan to do that? I am twice your size. And if you weren't aware, I only have one leg." Mark gave her a once over. She was much shorter than him and despite her curvy hips that were stirring something inside him, she was tiny. There was no way on Earth she could do it alone. "Plus who the Hell are you?"

Anya just rolled her eyes, "Anya, your new PT." She said as she grabbed a shower-chair and a pair of crutches. "We need to get your butt in gear, Mister. You need a hot shower and a good shave." She examined his face. "You also need a good protein meal, that will help you get your strength back and help you heal quickly. Let's get you cleaned up and then breakfast will be in when you are done." She hadn't really answered his first question, but when he tried to protest she gave him a look that told him she wasn't taking any of his shit. "You have holed up in this bed for the last few days." Pulling back the blankets he caught her wrist and glared at her.

"Who the fuck do you think you are? You have no fucking idea what I have been through the last month." Mark growled at her when she revealed his leg. It had finally healed enough he could be fitted for his prosthetic. He wasn't sure why he was doing what he was doing. He wanted out of the bed, but hadn't put forth any work to do it.

Anya wasn't expecting that from him, she met his eyes, "I do tho ugh..." she whispered, something made her falter with this man. The cold look in his eyes, the loss of hope. She hadn't seen that in a patient before. Biting her lip she sat on the bed beside him and took his hand. "You have gotta start trying."

Mark felt himself flip-flopping through his emotions. While he was royally pissed at this woman that he didn't even know, when she bit her lip and gazed into his eyes before taking his hand, he couldn't help but feel...something. Something that was not what he had been feeling the last few weeks\.This girl did not give him looks of pity, she gave him a look of determination and strength. A look that said she knew exactly what he was going through. She said she was his new therapist. She was very young. Mark thought she was just another nurse because of her scrubs.

"You need to get outta this bed...otherwise you are putting yourself at risk for getting a blood clot, bedsores, pneumonia." Anya stated flatly. "Do you really want to spend your entire life laying in a bed? Losing part of your leg is not the end of the world, no matter how close it might feel to that." Standing she grabbed the crutches. "Come on. What else do you have to lose by trying? You have everything to gain from it, nothing more to lose. Right?" Anya gave him a hearty smile as she stood and held out a hand to him. "I will do my best to get you out of here quickly. Trust me."

That short piece of advice really hit him hard. How was it that in 5 minutes of being with her he felt better than he had since he got to the hospital? Mark gave her a sharp nod in agreement, feeling a bit ashamed of himself for getting so low on himself when he should have been building himself up. Mark placed his hand in her's and gave a firm shake.

"That's what I wanted to hear!" She smirked.

Bandages & Scars

It took a good chunk of time, but Anya was able to get Mark standing using the crutches. He was panting heavily once he was able to finally even just stand up. A simple task drained him completely. The words of encouragement never ceased with Anya. After ensuring he was balanced, she assisted him into the shower-chair. All the while a crowd watched from the windows facing the nurses' station. Everyone was astounded that she had gotten him to do anything. Lisa smiled mischievously, she KNEW Anya would get him moving. The nurses whispered their astonishment in the quick turnabout in Mark. They wondered how it was that she was able to get him out of the bed so fast.

Lisa continued to smile, "I think there might be more to this." She noted the look Mark had when he first saw Anya. "I believe there may be some love at first sight workings going on." The thought pleased the older woman very much.

Anya gave Mark a few moments to regain his strength while she went to gather some supplies for him to use in the shower. Luckily he still had on a hospital gown so it would be easier for him to undress and shower without any help. Getting clothes on him would require some help from one of the aids. She was a bit confused when no one offered to assist her with the initial transfer. It didn't matter, she was able to do it herself anyway. Returning to his room with towels from the warmer and some toiletries, Anya grabbed one of the outfits his brothers had brought. She was curious to see how he felt once he had a hot shower and a good meal.

Mark sighed slightly as he gathered his thoughts while his therapist set up the shower room for him. He was just sitting here on some weird chair that looked like a bedside commode. He felt really embarrassed to be in this position. Then the thought crossed his mind. Was she going to help him shower? That was the last thing he wanted help with. But in the same notion, he would enjoy having her wash his back. He glanced up from the spot on the floor he was staring at to see her bending over in the closet where his personal belongings were. Damn. He thought and realized he was now staring at her ass. Then he noticed her shirt had risen in the back to reveal a small patch of deep scars on her spine. What had caused those? Aside from the scars and the fine shape of her ass, he also finally took notice to the half sleeve she was sporting on her right arm. Blues and greens swirled in a cosmic water pattern surrounding an intricate mermaid. Now that was cool. He did like women with tattoos. Lori never had any, said they weren't professional. He was now realizing how much of a stuck up bitch she was.

"Alrighty. I am going to get you in the shower, and leave you to it for as long as you need. A hot shower can really make you feel human again." She stated as she set everything on a small table near the wheel in shower. Everything would be accessible to him. "I will wheel you in and you can do your thing. I will look to see about breakfast then we are going to have OT fit you for your prosthetic today." Anya knelt down in front of him, not really taking much notice to the fact that he was completely bare under that thin fabric covering his manhood.

Given the nature of her job, Mark assumed this was no different than helping anyone else in the hospital. All professional. "What are you doing?" he questioned as to why she was kneeling between his legs. It wasn't until she held up some scissors that he realized what she was doing.

"I need to unwrap your bandages. I should make sure you are actually healed before I go hunting Margie down for the fitting." Anya made quick work of her task. It wasn't really her job to do wounds but it was quicker than calling for someone else to do it. She was more than capable. "Hm..." she examined the stump beneath his knee. "Honestly...I am surprised how well it has healed." She smiled up at him. "I get a lot of people who require a lot more time before they are ready, but you healed very well. Probably because you are young and fit." Or at least he was. He was a shadow of his former self. If only she had been able to see him before the accident. He still had some of his muscle but it had started to deteriorate.

Mark watched her examining his leg. She was way different than Lori had been. In all aspects. Lori was tall, dark haired, very fit, stern and cutthroat. Anya was the total opposite of her. The only thing they shared was their determination. Although Mark could tell Anya did it for the better of others, not like Lori who only thought of herself and how she would gain. "Try to give the skin on the upper area here a good scrubbin'." She showed him. "There is a lot of dead skin that we want to get rid of before we fit you." Standing back up with a slight grimace as she straightened her back. Mark frowned when he took notice. "A-also." she let out a soft, yet sharp breath." She went to his arm and unwrapped that as well, "This is pretty deep." Anya's soft fingers held his arm gently as she scanned over the deep wound from the second bullet that had bit him. "This will take awhile to heal, but it doesn't look infected." a small sigh of relief escaped her and she grabbed some plastic cling wrap. "But we don't want this to get wet, it can harbor bacteria."

"Anything else?" Mark asked a bit dryly. He honestly wanted to get this over with, increasing the embarrassment of being bathed by someone.

Anya walked around the chair and began to push him into the large shower room. "Nope, just pull that cord there if you need anything. I do a lot, but I ain't washing you." she gave a smirk. "You aren't an invalid."

Mark felt his lip twitch and a crooked smile formed, "But I thought I was getting special treatment?" He gave a fake pout. That was the first time he had laughed since he had been at the hospital. It also didn't help that his mind was having dirty thoughts about her already. He was a man after all, and she was attractive. Even if she wasn't the sort he had ever gone after. He preferred toned and tall, dark haired women and dark eyes for the longest time. Independent, strong willed, self sufficient, and self confident. Women like Lori. Anya was the opposite. While he imagined she was very strong willed and independent, she also seemed the type of woman who should have a man to keep her safe and protect her. Not to say she was weak, not in the slightest. Mark imagined she would love to be cuddled and held. To have a man to wipe away her tears and kiss her to make her feel better. Anya was not someone who hid her emotions. No. Anya wore them on her sleeve. Someone who didn't think she was in the same league as other women, never gave herself enough credit. That much he could gather. And it turned him on.

A Leg to Stand On

A nya stuck her tongue out, "Not from me, buddy I kick your ass, not wash it. Although I am sure I can ask Lisa or Eve to come bath you." she teased.

Letting out a shiver, Mark shook his head rapidly. That was the LAST thing he wanted. Anya pulled the curtain closed and gave him short instructions for the shower head before stepping out of the bathroom. Once she was gone, Mark turned on the shower as hot as it would go. It took him a few minutes to realize...he was still smiling. Anya was a firecracker. He knew the woman all of maybe 20 minutes but she made him feel motivated to do his best, but some of the dark thoughts still lingered. Pulling off the gown Mark allowed the water to wash over him. Oh yes. That did make you feel good again. He hadn't realized how disgusting he was until he finished scrubbing himself almost raw. After finishing he dried off the best of his ability. He was drained of most of his energy, and he still needed to dress.

Glancing around Mark grabbed a hold of the walls of the shower and used his foot to push the shower chair up to the sink. This was the first time looking at himself in the mirror, and he hardly recognized himself. The stubble he thought he had was a blooming beard. Something he never looked good with. Spying a razor, he made quick work of removing all of it before attempting to get dressed. It's just like standing on one leg. Mark told himself. He wanted to dress into at least a pair of boxers before he had help with his lower half. Not that he was shy. Luckily, he still had a good amount of arm strength to lift himself up and pull everything on. It took every last bit of energy he had to do so too.

"Mark?" A voice called out, "Are you doing okay?" Anya peeked her head in just as he pulled up his boxers, giving her a perfect shot of his still nice butt and a small amount of skin where his manhood rested. "AH! I'm sorry!" she removed her head, "I thought you would be covered! You got them on yourself?" Honestly she was surprised he had done so much with being as weak as he seemed from not eating or getting up out of bed enough. Why was she blushing so hard? It wasn't anything she didn't see on a regular basis, so why was it affecting her now? Maybe because she also got a good look at his now shaven face. He really was handsome underneath all that gruff.

Mark cleared his throat, he wasn't expecting her to peak in so suddenly. He was however proud that he was able to get semi dressed without calling for help. "You can come back in..." Pushing away from the counter he pat his face dry. Now he felt better.

Anya reentered the bathroom and Mark noted a hint of blush on her cheeks. So he affected her? The thought made him smile a bit "You got dressed on your own. That's awesome!" she smiled and helped him out of the bathroom. She wanted to help him finish, but the floor in the bathroom was wet. Big safety hazard, that she should advise him to be careful with next time so he didn't slip and crack his skull open.

"Well, the last thing I want help with is showering and dressing..." Mark said, a bit embarrassed.

"Understandable." Anya went to close the curtain to the windows that looked out to the hall near the nurses station. Luckily, all the nurses had gone back to their normal routine, but still gave side glances when they would pass by. Anya was a bit confused why they kept staring, and the weird smile on Lisa's face. "Your breakfast is here too." she motioned to the table. She had one of the aids go down to the employee cafeteria to get him something good to eat. Nothing motivated people better than a good meal.

Mark felt his stomach growl for the first time in days. He actually had a desire to eat today. "Hey...um..." Mark caught her by the wrist as she went to grab the pants he left in the bathroom. "I'm sorry for being rude..."

Anya blinked, a bit taken back by his apology. "Ah, forget about it...It happens. I mean...you went through some pretty brutal shit to lose that leg I'm sure." The warmth from his hand sent sparks through her. "You are allowed to feel the way you do." she continued, "But it's how you deal with it in the end; how you overcome it."

Mark shook his head, "That's not an excuse for treating you...and everyone else poorly for just trying to help."

"Everyone deals with pain and loss in different ways. No harm, no foul. I don't take things like that to heart. But thank you." Anya smiled softly at him. "Now. How about getting some pants on you. Unless you want to hang around in your undies all day?" She teased him.

Stretching a bit, Mark smirked, "You would like that, wouldn't you?" And that was when she was able to get a good look at the package he was sporting.

Dear God help her. She had helped many men her age before, so what was it about him that made her heat keep skipping like a 5 year old playing hopscotch. Swallowing she averted her eyes. "That is harassment!" she huffed trying to compose herself.

Wait a second...he was flirting with her. Why? He just had his heart ripped apart by Lori. What was wrong with him? Fuck that blushing look on her face was too cute to resist teasing. "Sorry, couldn't help it. I am usually a jokester." he shrugged.

"Hardy har har." Anya made a sour face and locked the wheels on his chair. "Come on, you can hold on to this while we get your pants on. Should be easy since they are sweatpants. Same as when you got everything else on." she instructed.

Mark was able to complete the task and Anya helped him over into a wheelchair before bringing him his breakfast. "Do you mind sitting with me awhile? Or do you have to go?" He asked.

"Nope, you are my only client. I was on vacation for the last week and a half, so all my patients are back home where they belong." Anya said with a hint of sadness. She had finally sent home a young boy she had been working with for the last 6 months. Sent him home...running. He cried, his parents cried, and she bawled. "I tend to take on a very small caseload so I can get to know my patients and work with them longer and get them home faster."

Taking a bite of bacon Mark watched her. "Sounds rough." he stated.

Shrugging a shoulder she shook her head, "It is what it is, but I am glad my patients all get to go home." Sitting on his bed she glanced out the window. "Your job sounds harder...A cop?"

Mark gave a bitter laugh, "Clearly...and I was good at my job...a junkie got the best of me. And an elderly woman." It pissed him off just thinking about it. Anya gasped. "I would give both legs if I could have saved her..." That was no lie. He wished he had been closer to stop the situation.

There was a long quiet silence, Mark wanted to keep eating but he felt the need to change the subject. "So...have you always lived in Chicago?"

"Uh huh, born and raised." Anya glanced back at him, "You?"

He nodded. Just then Margie came in and went over everything she needed to do to help get him ready for his prosthetic. Took measurements, and ideas of what exactly he wanted. Since he didn't have it yet and it would take time, Anya worked with him on things he could do without it. As well as working on getting his strength back with just basic exercises and weights. By the time the evening came, Mark was more exhausted than he had ever been in his entire life. Anya didn't allow him to rest for long in between activities. Seemed that she was not lying when it came to her approach in her treatments. Mark crashed, and hard. Got some of the best sleep too.

Battle Scars

That went on for a couple of weeks until he was able to wear his new leg and she started to help him walk.

Anya wrapped a gait belt around Mark's waist. "Seriously? What is with this thing..." Mark grumbled as he took notice of the hideous belt now around him before looking up at her glittering oceanic eyes. On top of his progress, he had also gotten to know Anya better. And it was safe to say, he really liked her company. Really liked her.

"Yes, hospital rules." Anya rolled her eyes. "Ready? We are going to stand, hold on to me if you need to steady yourself." She placed a leg between his and locked the wheels to his chair. Counting to three, Mark pushed up from the chair, her arms semi around him, hands looped around the gait belt to steady him. "That's it...perfect!" she smiled up at him. He had come so far, and it made her very happy to start seeing the darkness in his eyes starting to disappear.

Mark had his hands on her shoulders to keep steady on his wobbling leg. It would take some getting used to but he did enjoy the closeness of her at this moment. He could smell the soft scent of her shampoo tease his nose. He made the mistake of looking down as she looked up. For a short moment their eyes locked in a strange way. A way that made him want to kiss her.

"Try to take a step." she said softly, also feeling the heat rising between them.

Mark obliged and took a crooked step closer to her, his body brushing against hers. That was a mistake and it sent pain shooting through his leg. "Ah fuck!" Mark groaned and stumbled a bit.

Anya wrapped her arms around him to steady him from falling forward "Whoa there!" She backed him up quickly to the chair so he could sit. "I'm sorry...maybe I pushed you too soon." She knelt down in front of him and unhooked his prosthetic to check for injury. When she didn't find anything, she let out a sigh of relief. Working with phantom pains and nerve pain were very difficult sometimes. "Are you okay?" she asked, worried.

Mark blew out a breath and nodded, "Y-yea...just a spasm I think..." Shit. He was hoping to be able to do more, he liked seeing her smile when he achieved a milestone. "I'm okay..." he cupped her face and had her look at him.

Anya blinked in confusion at the somewhat intimate gesture. "Maybe we should take a break for today and just let you wear it before we have you stand again." She suggested as she stood back up and took a step back. "It's nice outside." she glanced out the window. "How about a trip outside? Some fresh air will do you some good. Plus it's lunch time."

"Sounds like a great idea." Mark nodded and slipped the prosthetic back on. It would take time, and at this point he was okay with it. It meant he would spend more time with Anya. Mark pulled the foot rests forward and used his arms to wheel himself. "Ready when you are."

Leading the way, Anya took Mark to her favorite spot at the hospital. A small garden where she tended to eat her lunch during the warmer months. "I love it here." Anya stated as they got to the spot with a bench.

Mark watched her closely. Watched the slight breeze make her hair float slightly and she took in a deep breath. The way the sun glistened and made her eyes shine a bright silver. He wondered what she looked like when she wasn't in scrubs. What she did on her days off. He bit his lip. "How did you get those scars on your back?" he asked finally.

"Huh?" Anya glanced out of her daydream and over to Mark. The last few weeks she had a lot of fun working with him. He was a very funny guy, but very serious too. He had taken his therapy head on since the moment she gave him his pep talk. No one ever asked about the scars, because not many saw them. When had he? "When did you?"

"That first day...when you grabbed my clothes. Your shirt rode up in the back and I saw them." Mark admitted.

Anya looked down at her hands and shifted slightly. "Remember when I told you I knew what it was like...to be in your position?" she noted his nod. "I was in a really bad car accident when I turned 18. I woke up a month later...hooked up to a bunch of machines...and I was paralysed." Mark stared at her, shocked, and she continued to tell him the story, all the way up until she graduated college and started working at the very hospital where she was treated. "They said I would never walk again. But I wouldn't believe them." She swung her feet and chuckled a bit. "I laid in the very same bed you did. Same room." she looked over at him.

"Damn..." Mark was never expecting to hear such a personal story. "Do they...do they still bother you?" He remembered seeing a twinged look on her face that day too.

"If I bend in certain ways, yea...The skin is tight. They itch in the winter...and they are ugly and deep." she admitted. "I have to avoid certain materials and I don't wear stuff that shows too much of my back...Tank tops push it."

"They aren't ugly." Mark's brows knit together at the very thought. Everyone had scars. So what if she had a few extra. They proved to be more like medals to show how far she had come. What she had overcome. Battle scars.

"Tell that to every guy I have dated since then." Anya clenched her jaw. Shit. She didn't mean to let that slip. It was still a weak point for her that caused dark thoughts to come back. The boy she had been dating at the time of her accident strayed away from her the month she was unconscious. Then really broke things off when he saw how bad the damage had been. Didn't want to be with someone who would be wheelchair bound forever. That had also fueled her desire to prove people wrong. Although she never told anyone that. Until now.

"Wait...what?" Mark shook his head in disbelief. It sounded the same as his story. Lori had left him at a vulnerable time as well.

"My boyfriend of 2 years left me after my accident...much like you." Anya shrugged. "Sorry...Lisa filled me in when I came back and took on your case."

"Word gets around in a hospital I guess." Mark glanced outward like she did. "For what it's worth...I think you look badass with those scars." Mark placed a hand on top of hers and gave a wicked smile.

Anya felt her heart leap into her throat and the touch and smirk he gave her. "They didn't look so 'badass' when they were red and inflamed." she said bitterly.

"Clearly I wasn't the one you were dating at the time." Mark said sharply. "I wouldn't have done that to you. Just like I doubt you would have done that to someone you loved. Seems like we just had shitty partners at a bad time in our lives."

"Yea...I wouldn't do that to someone. I just don't understand how someone could..." Anya's eyes showed a lot of emotion. It was clear to Mark that this was a really hard thing for her. And dear Lord he wanted to kiss her. Fuck.

"So you really do know what it's like to be in my position." He continued to keep his hand on hers. "Got hurt by the one who was supposed to stay with us and help us through it."

Anya nodded in agreement. "Life huh?" She smiled softly. She gave pep talks and shared some things with her patients. But never on this level. The feelings swelling inside her were very concerning. He was her patient. Falling for him was unethical and wrong. She had to do something to stop them. She would only end up getting hurt and hurting him in the process. Plus there was no way he felt anything for her. This was supposed to be strictly professional and she was pushing the limits. It didn't help that he was so easy to talk to, open up to.

Mark swallowed another question when he saw the conflicting stare in her eyes. She was battling something. He wondered what it could be. He would save more of the personal questions for another time. Maybe once he was able to walk and go home he would take her out on a date. A part of him rebelled against the idea, so soon after his breakup, despite it being close to 2 months now. The other part of him felt a stronger connection to her than he ever felt with Lori. Maybe it was lust and just a mutual passion they had shared. Maybe he never truly felt love for her either. The question was, would Anya go for half a man like him?

Anya sighed and inhaled a deep breath of fresh air. "I'm sorry you were treated like that." She said finally.

"Not your fault. She was a bitch and I didn't know it. Honestly, I am better off without a woman like her. Too bad it took 4 years to realize it. I think I need someone more sensitive...kind hearted, loyal, strong." Mark gave her a look that shouted, a woman like you.

A pit formed in her stomach. No. He was her patient. This was wrong.

Mark smiled at her, making her heart flutter once again. This was going to be a long few weeks.

Miracle Child

"You're looking better, Markie." Evan said as he set down a bag of clean clothes in his closet. "What changed so suddenly?"

Phil walked in a few moments later with their little sister. They had received a phone call from Lisa the nurse telling them about his amazing turn around in the last few weeks. So they thought it would be an excellent idea for him to see Maria.

"Just a PT who is kicking my ass." Mark smirked and then turned his attention to his little sister. "Minnie!" he smiled brightly and hugged her tightly when she rushed over to him.

"Mommy said you got a new leg!!!" Maria chirped happily and pointed to the prosthetic that he had finally gotten used to. "You look like a robot." she was surprised when she got a good look at it.

"I am part robot now!" Mark joked and tickled her. "Bring me to your leader!" he beeped like a robot, making her laugh loudly.

Evan smirked, "You seem happy. Did Lori come crawling back to you?"

Mark shot him a murderous look. Before he was able to reciprocate, someone else entered.

"Hey! Party in room 22!" Anya sing-songed as she jumped into the room.

The look on Mark's face when he saw her just answered the question Evan had been hounding. She was the reason. He had never seen that look in his brother's eyes before. Not even with his ex. So he had fallen for his therapist. How cliche and down right romantic. Evan gave his twin a look and a smirk. Phil noted the look as well.

Maria's lapis eyes widened brightly and her face lit up, "Markie! It's her!!! The pretty nurse with the long hair!" She pointed at Anya. "The one who smiled at me!"

"That pretty 'nurse' is a Physical Therapist, Anya. She is helping me learn to walk again." Mark smirked up at Anya. Taking not the blush that crept up her face. He picked small ways to flirt with her on a daily basis.

"Hi there, cutie pie! Good to see you again." Anya smiled happily at the little curly haired girl. She did remember seeing her a while ago. Her eyes and hair matched Mark's. If someone wasn't careful, she could be mistaken for his daughter.

"Mark, you should marry her! She is so pretty! And nicer than Lori." Maria made a sour looking face when she said Lori's name.

Everyone in the room, aside from Maria, was surprised. Children were always very honest and never held anything back. That didn't stop them from being a little shocked that she said that.

"Minnie, that's not exactly how it works..." Phil stated in order to break up the awkward silence. "You have to date someone before you can get married." He should not have said that.

Maria stopped her foot in frustration, "Uaggg! Fine! Anya! Go on a date with my big brother. He will treat you like a princess!" she decided. "Then you can get married and I can be the flower girl!!!" she skipped around pretending to toss imaginary flowers like she had practiced for MONTHS after Mark and Lori announced their engagement.

"OKAYYYY Time to go!" Evan picked her up and hugged his younger brother. "I promised this one ice cream before we sent her back to Mom."

And just like that Maria's mind went straight to ice cream. "YAYYY ICE CREAM!!!!" She cheered. "BYE MARKIE!" squealing as she waved, Evan still holding her.

Phil rubbed his neck, "Yea I should get going too...Oh! Before I forget." Fishing in his back pocket, Phil pulled out a cell phone. "Dad wanted me to give you this. In case you need anything...I stuck you on my plan for the time being. Anyway, I need to get home to my wife." Phil tossed him the phone, also mentioning the charger was in the bag of stuff they had brought him.

Mark thanked him as he left, leaving him and Anya in the room together. It wasn't abnormal for them to be alone together, but now his sister had pulled a stunt that left them feeling awkward.

"So...your family seems nice." Anya stated finally. "Twins? And a sister."

"Can't live without 'em. Yeah. Our parents got married really young, 18 and 19. Evan and Phil are identical twins. 18 months older than me. Minnie on the other hand...she was quite the surprise.

My mom was told she would never conceive again 5 years after I was born." Mark smiled softly, thinking about his little sister. "She had really bad endometriosis. They said it was a miracle she even had us 3. But then...on her 39th birthday she found out she was pregnant with Minnie. It was a hard pregnancy...ended up having a full hysterectomy during her c-section. Very unheard of."

Anya sat down on the chair beside him. "Wow...that's crazy..." she looked up at him and smiled though. "But I can see how much you love her, despite the large age gap."

Mark chuckled, "Yea, she always says I am her hero big brother. The other two were already out of the house and off at college. I stayed closer to home and went to the academy. It was cheaper that way."

"Well, it's clear she adores you." Anya admired him. "I always wanted a big family like that of my own one day." That is if she ever found a man who could get past the hideous scars that marked her back. She didn't even know if the accident had prevented her from carrying a baby.

"Same." Mark looked up at her from the side. "The bigger, the better." That smirk again.

"Well, we gotta get you out of here so you can go find you someone special to start popping out babies like a bunny. Not like Lo~ri." Anya mimicked Maria's snide sound of saying her name.

Mark bust out laughing. He loved her humor.

"Well, I just came to check on you before I head home for the evening." she stood. "Want anything special for tomorrow's buttkicking?" she asked in reference to food. She planned to have him walking more the next day.

"Surprise me." Mark raised a brow and gave a side smirk.

"Alright, rocky mountain oysters and goose liver." Anya teased. "High in protein."

They both just laughed and he watched her leave as well.

Mama Bear & Her Cub

"Yes! That's it!" Anya cheered.

Mark let out a shaky breath as he made it to the end of the walkway. He did it. It had been a long couple weeks, but Mark was making big strides. Literally. A lot of work managing his balance, his gait, and stamina. Anya had pushed him to the brink everyday. And he was grateful. They had started out inside the small walking area with bars. Today they were outside, the weather was beautiful yet again. All her encouragement and pushing got him down the entire walkway without stumbling once. She had stood there at the goal, cheering him on as he got up out of the wheel chair and made his way to her. He didn't even need the walker to help keep his balance.

He was also falling head over heels for her. She was his ultimate goal in the end.

Anya jumped up and down exclaiming her excitement. She was so proud of him for getting this far. "You did it! You made it, Mark!" she smiled brightly up at him. "All your hard work has paid off!"

Mark stared down at her. That smile he had come to look forward to every day when he woke up. The days she was off on the weekend killed him. He knew she couldn't be there everyday, but he had wished she could. So when she was smiling up at him like that, showing him how proud she was...he couldn't help but pull her into a tight embrace. In the past weeks, she showed him more emotion and genuine caring that Lori ever gave him in the 4 years they were together. Mark felt so many emotions welling up inside him. He had not only learned to walk again, and built back up his muscles to almost where they had been prior to his accident, he had repaired his heart. She repaired his heart. "I..." he clenched his teeth as he held her close, fighting back the tears that threatened him. He was trying so hard to keep himself strong. The way he always had. With Anya...he didn't mind feeling vulnerable, because he knew she wouldn't mind. In the same notion, he wanted to be strong for her. Wanted to share all these emotions with only her.

Anya's eyes widened as his arms wrapped around her. She didn't know what to do. Sure, many of her patients hugged her when they got to their end goal, but they weren't Mark. They didn't stir feelings and make her question her ethics as a medical profession. Then she felt the tears slip from his face and onto her collar bone. Crying? She had dealt with that too. Again...with Mark it was different. "M-Mark..." she breathed, feeling him shake slightly, as if he were fighting it. "I'm so proud of you." she whispered to him. "You don't have to hide your emotions."

That did it.

A heavy weight felt like it had released itself from his chest, and they remained like that for a long moment. Lifting a hand from around her back, Mark brought it up to her cheek. Fire erupted in her, she knew where this was going. Anya swallowed the lump in her throat. She should stop him. This was wrong. So wrong. But all she wanted in the world was for him to kiss her.

He held her gaze, his hot breath warming her lips. He was so close. "Anya...I.."

"Mark?" a female voice called out, preventing him from going any further.

Mark cursed softly and turned his attention to his mother. How could he forget it was Thursday. His parents decided to come visit him now that he was finishing up with his therapy. Anya hadn't had a chance to meet his parents yet, they both worked during the week and visited on the weekends when she was not at the hospital. "Hey mom." He smiled softly, although a little irritated she had kept him from finally telling Anya how he felt.

Diane blinked, cocking her head to the side at what she had witnessed. Mark had a girl in a very loving embrace. "Hi, honey. Sorry we are early. Ray got off early so we could come see you." Diane made her way up to them in the garden.

"Where is Dad?" Mark questioned, not seeing the man. "And Minnie?"

"Talking to the nurse about your discharge. Maria is at a birthday party." Diane turned her attention to Anya who was looking very embarrassed and flustered. "Hi, I'm Diane, Mark's mother." She gave Anya a head to toe look. She looked familiar.

Anya felt a bit of relief when she heard that it was his mother. A part of her was almost scared that it was Lori. But that was just absered. Mark looked way too much like this woman. Same piercing blue eyes and chestnut hair. "I'm Anya, Mark's physical therapist." she blushed, shaking the woman's hand. Yes. She was his PT so why was she allowing him to nearly kiss her? She saw the clouded look that passed over his mother's eyes. A look that said she had just seen what had almost happened. A look that said don't mess with my son, or I will tear you to pieces. The last thing Diane wanted was for her son's heart to be broken. Again. "I should go. I will let you guys have some time together." Anya looked up at Mark. "I will be in my office for a while...I have to work on your discharge paperwork." she gave Diane a big smile before heading back to her office.

Staring at her as she walked away, Mark sighed too loudly.

"What is with that sigh?" Diane raised a brow at her son, still oblivious to the fact that he was standing on his own. She watched the longing look in his eyes. "Mark?"

Mark shifted his gaze to his mom. "Sorry...I just..."

"I know that look." Diane narrowed her eyes. "You are in love with her."

"Mom!" Mark shot at her.

"You cannot fool me. I have never seen you look like that, but I know that look. It's the same one your brothers had for each of their wives. The same look your father gets when he looks at me."

"Nothing gets past you does it?" Letting out a sigh of defeat he gazed back at where Anya had been. "I do. At least...I think I do. I can't explain it...I never felt like this with Lori..."

Diane frowned, "Mark...I don't want you to get hurt again."

"Anya isn't like Lori."

"Does she like you back?" Her brows furrowed, folding her arms over her chest.

"I...I don't know. Maybe? I feel like she does but it's almost like she is fighting it. She always smiles around me, blushes when I pick at her or flirt." Mark never hid anything from his mother. They were really close.

"Mark..." she warned.

There was no arguing with the woman once her mind was made up. Mark pretended to scratch his back. "Hungry?"

"Starving. We brought chinese. You said you wanted some." Diane appreciated the change in subject.

Mark was honestly glad they came, he needed to figure out his game plan for when he returned home. He really didn't want to go back to that condo. "Come on, let's go find Dad." Mark began to lead the way, waiting on his mother to finally realize the most important thing.

"YOU ARE WALKING!" she exclaimed finally, making Mark chuckle.

"'Bout time you realized I have just been standing here. Even in shorts." Mark teased. "You can thank Anya." He threw back at her as he continued on.

The two made their way back inside to find his father. He was talking to Lisa and Eve. "Hey Pops." Mark called out to get his attention.

The older man turned, shocked to see his son upright and walking. Almost back to his former glory. Minus a leg. "Mark! Look at you!" he smiled proudly.

Together they had their dinner in the small eating area for the rehab unit. "So, I want to get rid of the condo. I can't live there after all this." Mark stated as they ate.

"But it's such a nice place." Ray started, but his wife gave him a death glare.

"I know, Dad. It's just too much to go back to. 4 years. Gone just like that." Mark rubbed his temple. "I know it sounds pathetic. Plus I can get a good price for it right now with the market the way it is." He had done some research lately, because he knew he wasn't going back there. "I will need some help packing...and I might have to stay with you guys until I can find a new place." The last thing he ever thought he would have to do was move back home at 26. Temporary or not. "If that's ok."

"Of course it's okay!" Diane huffed. "How could you even say such a thing! We will get everything packed up and put into storage for you as soon as possible. Your brothers will be more than enough help." Ray just nodded in agreement with his wife. He also knew better than to argue with the woman.

"Thanks...I will start contacting an agent to get it listed. I will be here for a few more days while everything is finished up with my rehab. OT still needs to clear me to drive again." Losing a leg was one thing, but he had lost his right one. That made things a little more tricky. He had to relearn how to drive again too.

Under Your Scars

After dinner they walked Mark back to his room and said their goodbyes. He was really looking forward to getting out of a hospital setting. He missed his real bed more than anything.

Lisa was at the nurses station near his room and watched his parents leave before she hobbled her way over. "Can I talk to you?" she asked, not really giving him an option before she motioned for him to enter the room.

"What's up?" Mark asked in confusion. Something seemed a little off about her attitude this evening. "Is something wrong?"

"It's about Anya." Lisa pulled up a chair and sat down. Mark gave her a puzzled look. "Are you serious about her?"

"How did you...How does everyone know?!" Mark ran a hand through his hair and turned away from her. He needed a haircut. "Is it seriously that obvious?"

"You may as well walk around with a neon sign attached to you." Lisa smiled deviously. "Look. Anya..." she paused, thinking of the words she wanted to express, "Anya is special, and she requires someone who isn't going to go running away from her at the sight of...well things that have happened to her." She wasn't sure how she wanted to word what she was saying.

"Do you mean the scars on her back?" Mark looked back at her from the window. "She already told me the whole story."

"They don't bother you?" Lisa sounded astonished.

"Not in the slightest. I mean...damn I have one fucking leg and she doesn't look at me with pitty or...or shame." He growled the last word, mind lingering on Lori. "She treats me like a whole man."

"She likes you, you know." Lisa adjusted her glasses on her face. "A lot. And it scares her. Anya has been hurt badly by men in her life since her accident."

Mark felt his stomach turn at the thought that she felt the same way. That was good news, but he was also concerned that she was scared of her feelings. All because of her past relationships. "I would never hurt her."

Lisa gave him a look of worry. Anya was like a daughter to her, and while she would not reveal some of the more personal things about her to Mark they burned on her tongue as a warning. "She is innocent, kind, and a little naïve. But damnit is she strong."

"Lisa. I love her." Mark admitted. "I know I do. I thought I loved Lori, but it's clear it was just lust. With Anya, it feels so much different. Like this...primal need to protect her." He watched the look of worry disappear from Lisa's face and become replaced by a smirk.

"Just know Hell will rain down if you hurt her." She struggled to stand and then made her way out of the room. "Make sure you tell her soon. Time is running out."

Mark let out a shaky breath. How was he going to tell her? He stood in his room for several moments before he made a hasty escape, hoping she was still in her office. He noticed the smile on several of the nurses' faces as he went. He really needed to figure out a better poker face. It was a time like this when he wished he could run again. Maybe in due time. Going as quickly as his body would let him, he made his way up to Anya's office. Relief swept over him when he saw she was still there. He loved the way she almost looked mad when she was concentrating, how today she had her hair up in a long ponytail, how she was chewing her lip and tapping away at her keyboard. She was beautiful. "Anya." He knocked to announce his presence.

Anya jumped a bit, not expecting someone to come see her. Her expression softened when she saw who it was. "Mark." she breathed. There was something in the look he was giving her. "I was just finishing up some paperwork for your discharge." She stood and stepped around her chair. "Is there something I can help you with?" her hands fidgeted with the back part of the chair as she gazed up at him. There had been a small part of her that hoped he would come to see her before she left for the evening. Especially after the moment that had been interrupted by his mother. Another part of her brain began to panic if he did come to her and someone just happened to catch them. There was something there between them. She wanted to know what it was, and hoped it was real. Of course her paranoid brain just kept whispering it would just end up the same way as the others. And that hurt.

"As a matter of fact, there is." Mark closed the already small gap between them. Taking her face in his hands he kissed her.

A small squeak escaped her and her eyes widened. She had not expected that so quickly. It felt nice. Her eyes fluttered shut and she fell into the kiss, trying not to let her knees go completely weak. He was still learning to do things with his new leg. Anya was actually quite proud that she was able to even think with the way that kiss made her feel.

As she wrapped her arms around his neck, Mark deepened the kiss, allowing his tongue to dance with hers. She tasted sweet against his, like she had been eating fruit. Pushing her up against the back desk, Mark lifted her up and placed her on top. Anya gasped a little at the suddenness, and the fact that he lifted her with such ease.

He couldn't stop himself. They were soft and the gasp she gave allowed him to deepen the kiss.

Anya gave little protest in the first few seconds, but then pushed him away. "W-what are you doing?!" she panicked, looking around to ensure no one witnessed what had just transpired. "I-If someone saw me! I-I could lose my license!" Her heart rate was already elevated from the kiss, then went full throttle when she began to imagine what would happen if they had been spotted.

Mark stared down at her. He just jeopardized her job because he couldn't keep his hands to himself until it was the end. "Anya...I'm sorry...I just...I've fallen in love with you." He admitted.

The look of panic on her face changed quickly. He saw the look of shock and a small amount of longing in her eyes before it transitioned back to panic. "M-Mark...I'm your physical therapist...it...it's wrong..." She really wished her brain would stop switching from wanting him to kiss her and thinking of what would happen if they were found like this.

She hadn't actually denied him, and that gave him a small amount of hope. "What's so wrong about it? We're both consenting adults?" Mark honestly didn't see the issue. It wasn't like he was an invalid and she was taking advantage of him.

Anya bit her lip, trying to calm herself. "It...it's a moral and ethical guideline we must follow...to be intimate with a patient...it....it's frowned upon. I could get fired...or worse."

"Well...how long do I have to wait?" Mark questioned.

"Mark this...why?" Anya didn't know what else to say. She was almost speechless. He said he loved her. While it made her happy to hear he had feelings for her that gave her some hope, it also scared her to death. This job was her life. She wanted nothing to ever jeopardize it. This whole thing made her head spin.

Mark sighed and looked up, still keeping the distance between them small. If it weren't for her panic, he wanted people to see. "You are real." he shrugged, "I don't know how the Hell to explain it. You just...you just stir these feelings in me. I thought I was in love with Lori, but being with you made me realize I didn't love her." He paused. "Well...not like this."

"You are vulnerable...this is a hard time for you. I was nice...an-"

Mark cut her off by kissing her again. "Tell me you don't feel it too. I've seen you blush when you look at me." he let out a gruff, sexy purr.

The sound sent a shiver through her body. He saw right through her. The battle of emotions was crippling. She wanted to give in and be able to tell him she felt the same, but it seemed impossible. "Please...don't do this..." She felt a tear slip down her cheek. How could she choose between a man who showed her a genuine interest, knowing her past and her scars, and the place where she belonged.

"Anya!" A stern voice called behind them.

~Sorry those who have read this part, I redid it...I wanted more drama~

A Little Favor

"Anya!" A stern voice called behind them.

Oh no. No no no! Anya's eyes widened. Someone had seen them. And not just anyone. The director of the department.

Mark turned around, his back to the man who had called out.

Panic surged once more, "M-Mr. Kennedy..." her voice broke. She was done for.

"My office." he turned on his heel and stormed away.

Mark never let go of her, there was a strong, deep seeded urge to protect her. This was his fault.

The tears slipped from her eyes, "I am going to lose my job." she said flatly as she watched her boss make his way to his office.

Anya shook and pushed away from him before running to try and plead her case.

Mark stood there watching her go, cursing himself. What had he done?

"M-Mr. Kennedy...p-please it...it isn't what it looked like." Anya began the moment she burst into the office.

"Well, from where I was standing, you didn't do much effort to push him away." His eyes narrowed. "You took advantage of the situation between you two. How far has this gone?" He began to hound.

"No...I..."

"Well from the reports I have gotten...he had been pretty close to you for the last few weeks. Giving him some...special treatments?" Mr. Kennedy looked up from a report sitting on his desk.

Anya yelled finally, "NO! There has been nothing else! I-I swear.. .please...don't fire me..." The sheer look of terror on her face begged him.

Mr. Kennedy snorted, "Relations between a patient and a provider are strictly prohibited. I'm sorry. But we have to let you go." a devious smirk played on his lips.

And just like that. Anya's world shattered. "N-no..." No longer frozen in her tracks she turned to run.

"Unless." He started.

Anya paused and turned her head.

"You show me how sorry you are." Mr. Kennedy made his way around the desk to her. He cupped her face and spun her around, making her gasp.

"W-what..."

A dark chuckle escaped him and he trailed his thumb over her lip. Cupping her bottom he pulled her close and allowed her to feel his erection. "I have a few ideas of how you can repent. And I won't fire you." He kissed at her neck and held tighter as she squirmed against him. Another chuckle brushed against her neck as his hand trailed up to grope her breast. "Do this little favor for me and never speak to him again. All will be forgiven."

"N-No! Let me go!" Anya gasped and pushed. He was too strong.

"ENOUGH!" a voice yelled out in anger. "YOU GET YOUR FILTHY HANDS OFF HER!" Mark huffed as he pushed his way into the room, others were following suit. Mark grabbed the man by the back of the neck and threw him to the floor. "Don't you dare lay a finger on her!" Mark punched him.

Several of the other female staff members stood glaring at their boss, arms crossed over their chests. Anya stared at them all, wide eyed. "W-what?"

Lisa rushed over to Anya and pulled her into a hug as she caught up on what had just transpired. "My sweet naïve child, he has been after you for months...thank God you never realized his intentions. He does this to half the female staff. Now we finally have proof." Lisa stroked her hair and held her close, glaring daggers into Kennedy. It hurt her they held Mark back until the last second in order to get it recorded for evidence. She was just thankful Anya was okay.

Apparently, Mr. Kennedy was the type of man who threatened women's jobs if they didn't fuck him. He was subtle about it for a while, and no one had gone forward in fears that if they tried to come out, they would be fired anyway. Plus there had never been any evidence. But they had all seen what he had done to Anya.

The hospital security had come to cart him away and everyone went back to work after giving their reports to the cops.

Anya stood in a corner, rubbing her arms as she continued to watch everything. Well...watch Mark talk to some of the officers. It seemed like he knew them by the way they talked. She had no idea things like this had been going on. Maybe she had been blind to his advances the last few months. It made sense, she was always engrossed in her work. She just wanted to go home and take a hot shower.

Mark finished with a nod to Chase and Elliott before making his way back to Anya. "Hey..." he said as he closed the distance between them.

"You are walking." Anya said softly. "Looks like my treatments really are done." She wasn't expecting him to be walking around this much.

"Sheer willpower and anger." Mark laughed with an exhausted breath as he sat beside her, but then got really serious again. "Any a...I...I'm so so-"

This time Anya cut him off by wrapping her arms around him and kissing him.

Everyone stopped and stared, the staff, the other patients, even the cops. It was like something from a romance movie. Her hands cupped his face and she stared up into his gaze, "I love you too." she breathed once the kiss broke. "I will make it work...I won't let them fire me over it." The fire still burned behind her eyes. That determination he had come to love in her.

"Anya." Mark smiled.

Everyone around them clapped and cheered. Lisa especially. That sparkle in her eye. They weren't going to let anything happen to

Anya. And that was exactly what happened when the higher ups came sniffing around in question as to what had really gone on. Everyone had pleaded her case, not allowing love to be squished by a simple form of semantics.

Laughter Heals Wounds

S everal days later...

Mark was finally discharged. His family had come to support him, his brother even brought his car. All the nurses and therapists came as well. Anya rushed in, worried she had missed his farewell. She was happy to see he had waited for her. The night he had confessed, Mark had given her his phone number and they had begun to text. With those messages, Mark got to know her even more.

"Sorry I'm late." she said in a hushed tone as he came up to her. "There was an accident by my apartment and I couldn't get out." she caught her breath.

"No worries, I knew you would come." Mark brushed a strand of her hair from her face. "Can I see you this evening?" He questioned.

Anya felt her face heat up and people began to notice their soft whispers to each other. "Tonight?" He nodded to her. "O-okay." her stomach did a flip as she agreed to go out with him. She hoped she never stopped feeling this gitty around him, it made her too happy.

"I will pick you up. Send me the address." Mark turned to head back to his family. As much as it pained him to do it, it was going to take time to sell his condo. He really didn't want to go back there, but in the same notion, he really did not want to stay with his parents. Not if he really wanted to have private time with her, even if they were not going to be intimate just yet. As much as he wanted to. Mark wanted to handle her with the utmost care and respect, because she deserved nothing less.

Anya paced her apartment after work, racking her brain on what to do and what to wear. He hadn't given much indication on where he was planning on taking her. Why did it seem like dates always went this way? No idea what to expect, because the guy wanted to be spontaneous and fun. Since he didn't seem like the type to go somewhere fancy, Anya decided to go with a pair of shorts and a flowy tank top. Rooting through her panty drawer she also made sure to match a cute pair of lace underwear and a black bra that gave her a good amount of cleavage. Amaya had always said it made her boobs look good whenever they went out on the weekends. It was a time like now she really wished her roommate hadn't gone and gotten married and moved out. But after her accident it had been hard for her to stay in the apartment. Anya left her hair down long to keep some of the scars on her shoulders from peaking through. Despite what Mark said, she was still a little embarrassed about them.

Not giving her a moment to second guess her choice of outfits, there was a loud knock on the door. "I'm coming!" Anya called out as she slipped on her flip flops.

"If I have anything to do with it, you will be." Mark joked as she opened the door.

"OH YOU!" Anya playfully punched his arm and smiled. She really enjoyed his humor. It was nice to see him acting more like himself as time had gone on. Tucking a strand of hair behind her ear, Anya suddenly felt a little nervous. Her eyes started at his feet and went up to meet his eyes. Even having a prosthetic, he looked damn good. It honestly made him that much hotter. At least in her opinion. It was the way he carried himself.

Mark was dressed in a pair of dark grey cargo shorts and a black Sabaton band shirt. Casual was the way to go. Mark smirked and pulled her to him. "Hello beautiful." he kissed her breathlessly.

"Hi." Anya gave him a hazy look. The way he kissed her made her feel almost high. The scent of him was intoxicating. He smelled crisp and manly. She was not sure how to describe his scent. Just him.

"Ready to go?" Mark tipped her chin up to gaze down into her eyes, then traveled lower. He liked seeing her in casual clothing. He really liked the shorts she had decided to wear. With how active her job was, despite having a very curvy body, her legs and arms were well toned. Mark couldn't wait to see what hid beneath.

How was it that he went so long living across the street from her and never once saw her? Anya showed him her apartment. It was older compared to his, but was homey. "Wait a second..." Mark looked around. "Do you know Amaya?" He questioned. "She lived over here."

Opening the door she glanced back, "Yea, she was my roommate. ..she got married to a cop recently. How do you know Ama?"

Mark ran a hand through his hair, "I work with Zane!" Small world. "I had no idea you were her roommate."

"Oh wow...." Anya laughed.

"I was actually the one who found her location...when she was kidnapped."

Anya's eyes widened as he told her how he found her from a live stream video the cult had posted on social media. "That's amazing, Mark. You seriously saved one of my best friends." That deepened her appreciation for him all the more.

"Nah...that was all Zane running in there guns ablazing." Mark laughed at the images of Zane rushing in like a knight in swat gear. A dark part of him was a bit envious now. There would be no missions like that for him anymore.

"Mark?" Anya placed a small hand on his cheek and looked up at him. He still got that cloudy look in his eyes from time to time. It was something she understood, there were days when she got it as well.

"I have a special place I am taking you tonight." Mark said, shaking off the negative plague that threatened him.

Mark took Anya to a small little hole in the wall place that he had discovered while he was still in high school. He swore they had the best burgers he ever had, and during the evening they had live shows and stand up. He was happy when Anya was all for it. Even more happy when he found out that she knew of his favorite band, Sabaton. Swedish power metal. The woman was full of surprises, especially when she started to sing along to prove to him she knew who they were. Lori never appreciated his taste in music, thought music was just a waste of time.

Anya was beyond happy the entire time, they spent the evening at the burger joint, listening to a local comedian doing his skit. Mark couldn't keep his eyes off of her, and how big her smile was the whole night. She had one mixed drink, and had gotten all bubbly and happy. He was starting to realize just how boring his life had been while he was with Lori. It also pissed him off that he kept thinking about her, no matter that it was negative. Mark used to have fun and go out, but that slowly started to stop after he got engaged. Which reminded him, he needed to return that ring he had spent a small fortune on. Add that to the list of shit he needed to get done sooner rather than later.

As the show came to a close Anya rested her head on Mark's shoulder and let out a happy sigh from all the laughter she had produced. "That was great." her hand interlaced with his. She hadn't had this much fun in awhile, work had engulfed her, and with Amaya out of the apartment she didn't really have anyone to sit and make random plans with.

"I'm glad you enjoyed it." He kissed the top of her head.

"I've been on a few dates, but nothing this fun." Anya giggled a bit, thinking about the comedian again. "It's getting late. Do you want to go back to my place?" she didn't look up at him, just kind of trailed her thumb over the top of his hand. She didn't want to part ways with him just yet.

~If ya'll have never heard Sabaton, you should totally listen to them. Their music is really cool, very different type of metal. Their music tells historic stories~

Warmup

"It's getting late. Do you want to go back to my place?" she didn't look up at him, just kind of trailed her thumb over the top of his hand. She didn't want to part ways with him just yet.

Now that was something he was not expecting. "Sounds good." Mark purred in a husky tone. Taking the opportunity Mark took her by the hand and led her out to his car. They joked about the show all the way back to her apartment, sharing funny stories that happened to each other while they grew up. "I honestly don't know where they come up with that stuff." Mark cracked up as he followed her inside the darkened apartment. His curiosity peaked when she turned on the lights. He hadn't got a good look at the inside when he picked her up.

The apartment, despite being 2 bedrooms, was relatively small. Being a rental, he imagined that she wasn't allowed to do much as far as decor and paint, but it was very nice inside. Clean and minimally decorated.

"Welcome to my humble abode." Anya set down her bag and kicked off her flip flops. She made her way over to a bookshelf near the TV, "This is Oscar, my goldfish." She smiled brightly and made a fish face at the fat goldfish swimming around in a small bowl. Anya worked long hours and her apartment didn't allow 'pets'. The last carnival that had blown through town, Anya and Amaya had gone and she won him as a prize. Honestly, it surprised her that he was still alive and thriving.

Mark blocked his mouth, snorting slightly. Failing miserably at hiding his reaction. That was probably the cutest thing he saw her do. Coming up behind her, Mark wrapped his arms around her waist and pulled her close to him.

Anya let out a sleepy sigh and relaxed against him. "Thank you for such a wonderful night." she allowed her tiny hands to run over his hairy arms, enjoying the warmth that radiated from him.

"You deserved it. I feel like I can really be myself around you. Like listening to my favorite music without question, go see funny shows, and just relax. It's only been one night...how is it that you can make me so comfortable in such a short time than I did in a 4 year relationship?"

She remained quiet for a moment, unsure of how to respond. It was just natural, how could you be anything other than yourself in a relationship? "I dunno...I wouldn't have it any other way. We have so much in common." She turned in his arms to face him. "I feel the same though." Standing on her tiptoes, "I can be myself." she muttered just before their lips met.

Mark was engulfed in the feel of her soft lips pressing against his. This is who he should have been with from the get go. She was perfect.

"Spend the night with me." Anya said softly as she broke away, remaining only mere inches from his face. She bit her lip. There. It was out. Anya wanted this, and she didn't care if it seemed too soon. People did this sort of thing all the time. It felt right. Everything about him felt right.

Whoa.

Mark stared at her for a long moment, processing what she just told him. Mark had hoped he could work her up to this moment in due time, but this was quite a shock. "Are you sure?" He felt like he was just gawking at her. The last thing he wanted was for her to have any second thoughts, because he sure as Hell wouldn't. She nodded and backed away, holding his hand as she led him to her tiny room. Mark felt himself instantly harden.

Watching her take a deep breath, Anya pulled off her shit, exposing her back completely to him. He had only seen the lower half of her back, never the full extent of the scarring. It was bad. It was no doubt that it would still be a cause of pain or irritation at times; depending on how she moved. Mark said nothing to her, just walked closer and placed a hand on her back. "You're beautiful."

Anya felt tears welling up in her as he trailed his fingers over her scars. No one had ever told her that they accepted her scars. It seemed so minor, but to her it was a big deal. But there was something else about her that always came up during her relationships. Scars could be ignored if she were laying on her back. "Mark...I've...I have never had sex..." she blurted. "M-my ex...we tried...and the foreplay...it ended badly." Her ex tried to ignore the scars for a little while, but when he touched her she never had an orgasm. He tried for a while before giving up. Anya just didn't want to continue after the frustration and embarrassment. Their relationship ended very shortly after that. "I...I think it had to do with my accident. Messed things up."

Mark was not expecting that from her. "Hm..." a devious smirk crossed his lips. "I doubt that very seriously." He pulled her close and pressed against her, hearing her gasp. "I just don't think he was doing it right...he had something else on his mind besides bringing you pleasure. Or your mind forced you to believe you were messed up, because he wasn't the one." His lips caught hers for a sensual kiss before he moved down to her neck, hands exploring her body. "You are already responding well to my touch."

Mark pulled Anya back to him and his lips claimed hers. It was heated, full of passion and need. Holding on to him tightly, she felt herself spark to life. Slow. He needed to take this slow. Mark continued to repeat that in his head. Pulling off his shirt he watched her bright eyes darken with desire. His hands trailed her and he felt her go rigid for a moment. He watched her shake away the bad thoughts that had started. Mark knew in time, she would not even think about them when he stripped her. Taking that opportunity, his skilled fingers snapped her bra hook apart. Small scars marked her bountiful chest and a few spots on her stomach. He noted them and dismissed them as he gave all his attention to her breasts. Removing her bra and tossing it to the side, Mark heard a soft moan escape Anya.

Much better.

Before he knew it he was pressing her nude body onto the bed. Mark stood before her, just looking at her. She was so beautiful. In so many ways. Her pale skin flushed under his careful touch and her nipples peaked as he gave them his full attention.

Anya blushed under his heated gaze and swallowed. She wondered what was going through his head. Even though he was tasting her and rubbing her chest, his gaze continued to meet hers. The way he was eating her up with just his eyes made her tingle all over. Especially between her legs. A place she thought had remained dormant since her accident. It only took minutes before she was a panting mess.

Sitting at the edge of the bed, Mark removed his prosthetic and smirked when he felt Anya's soft skin wrapping around him in an embrace. They both needed patience and understanding. They found it in each other. He returned his attention to her and pressed her back onto the bed beneath him. Settling himself between her legs he kissed all the way down her body. "I will prove to you..." Mark started as he trailed his fingers over her inner thigh. "You are capable of feeling pleasure." He noted the wide eyed look Anya gave him right before his tongue slipped over her hot sex.

Anya's body reacted immediately to him and she moaned. She felt him smirk against her and keep going. It felt as if her body was on fire, "Oh Mark!" She felt herself gripping the blankets. The sight of him between her thighs was tortuous alone. His tongue was its own deadly sin. A temptation she wasn't sure she could deny.

Mmm. Perfect. Mark thought proudly. The way her body opened up for him, accepted his touch, he loved it. The cute little whimpers that were escaping her as he pushed her closer and closer to the edge. Slipping a finger inside, he felt her start to really melt against him. Mark slid another in with ease, thanks to how wet she had become just from his tongue teasing her relentlessly. His name came out in a blissful cry of pleasure. Riding her down from her orgasm he kissed his way back up. "What was that you were saying?" he teased.

Anya managed to make a pouty face. "N-not funny." she panted. Her body was humming with pleasure. That was incredible, and reassuring. She didn't know she was able to achieve such an amazing feeling.

~Hey ya'll, sorry the last three chapters are different. I wanted to redo them and add a little extra drama to the story for shits and giggles. Don't want things being too stale :3 Anyway. Thank you all who have continued to read and leave awesome comments. That really drives me. I have been in a funk lately where I desperately wanna write, but words will not come out. I am a full time nurse and things are chaotic. I want this story finished so I can have my closure on it as well as work on Irish Dreams and a few other ideas I have floating around. Possibly even a sequel to Mafia Doctor~

Perfect Timing

Mark hovered above her, admiring her. "God you are so fucking beautiful..." he smiled and cupped her face. Then he felt her push at his boxers. She wanted more, and he was happy to give her exactly what she wanted. Mark assisted her in pulling them down, and he noticed her swallow as she saw his stiff manhood.

It was one thing to see patients, who typically were flaccid. Not Mark, he was hard and ready for her. She felt nervous. It was her first time, but she wanted nothing more than to be with him. Anya pulled him back to her, craving his closeness again. Their lips met, this time softly and careful as Mark began to slide the head of his cock into her warm sheath. His hands tangled in her hair as he continued into her, his lips working at hers. It took his breath away when he finally pushed past her barrier and he was fully inside.

"A-Are you ok?" He asked in a shaky breath. It felt good. Too good. For him. Women's first times tended to be a different story.

"Yes...oh God yes." Anya panted. It had only hurt a pinch, plus she was still feeling warm and fuzzy from her orgasm.

Mark gave silent thanks inside his head. Working her up before-hand had really helped ease her. Rocking his hips, Mark increased his pace. Her taut nipples teased at his chest and he couldn't help but suck and nip at them again. That just made the whimpers and moans that came from her more needy and sweet. Her body was so responsive to him. It didn't take much longer for him to reach his breaking point. Letting out a deep groan he came hard. Harder than he ever had with any woman he had been with. Not even his first time on Prom night with his high school girlfriend. Never like this with Lori, no matter how hot and fiery their sex had been.

He laid connected to her for several long moments. "Anya..." He whispered and kissed her. "Fuck...you feel so damn good."

Anya looked up at him, her breathing returning back to normal. "Y-You too..." she blushed.

Mark laughed at her reply and pulled out of her. He froze. "Fuck..."

Anya cocked her head confused.

"I...I didn't wear a condom."

Anya had a mild bit of panic surge through her and she counted in her head, "No...it should be okay...I am in a safe period." she reassured him, remembering her period just ended days before. There was also the small inkling she might not even be able to get pregnant even if it had not been safe.

That wasn't something she wanted to think about after such bliss. Another day.

Mark let out a sigh of relief. "I'm sorry...I should have been more careful." While he wanted kids, it was way too soon. He relaxed beside her, pulling her into a spooning embrace. They remained quiet for a long while. "I didn't mean that in a bad way. I want kids...it's just too soon. I want to be with you first...get to know you better." Anya had gone quiet. He wasn't sure if he had said something wrong. Mark glanced at her back, in this position he was able to see just how bad the extent of her scars were. He swallowed a lump that was forming. "Anya?" That was like putting a potato in a tailpipe. He felt like he just ruined their romantic evening

"I know. I didn't think you meant it in a bad way." She glanced up at him, turning to lay her head on his chest. "Sorry, I was just enjoying the feel of you holding me." Anya gave him a smile.

Maybe he hadn't ruined it after all.

"I love you." Mark kissed her.

"I love you, too." She admitted. Some might say it is too early to say you are in love with him. To Hell with what others thought. This was her life, and Mark made her happy, and felt things she never knew she could feel. In her heart...and parts much lower.

~Sorry for the short chapter, but I wasn't really sure how to extend it more~

Spotlight

L abor Day weekend....

Anya let out a tired huff as she slammed the trunk of Mark's car. They were going on their first vacation together. Not only were they going together, they were meeting up with Mark's entire family for their annual camping trip for Labor Day weekend. Anya had only met his parents and siblings, this time she was meeting his entire extended family. Although his father, brothers, and of course Maria, love Anya from the beginning...Mark's mother was still hesitant about the entire relationship. Anya didn't blame her, since he had been her patient and some people were still questioning the ethics behind it. Diane was still civil to Anya. Thank goodness.

Letting out a small sigh as she took a moment before going back inside the apartment. Anya hoped in time that the woman would come to like the idea of Anya and Mark being a couple. It would take time, especially after Lori. The name still made her blood start to boil. If she ever met the woman, Anya wasn't sure what she would possibly say or do.

Mark stepped out onto the landing and glanced down at his girl-friend who seemed to be lost in thought. It had been a few months since he left the hospital and started dating her. This trip was very big for his family since he was a kid and he was not the least bit nervous about bringing Anya along. Lori always hated these trips and was a drama queen the entire weekend. They always ended up leaving early because 'the bugs were eating her alive.' Mark snorted and shook his head. Their relationship had been boring as fuck. Anya was excited for the trip. Mark glanced away from Anya who was checking something in the back seat and looked at his prosthetic. This was going to be a real trial. Hiking and walking around the campground...and a special place he wanted to take Anya behind the waterfall. Mark had gone back to work and was doing some stuff back in the streets of Chicago, but not like he had. Now he had a partner as well.

Mark took note that everything inside the apartment was going to be safe. Oscar the fish would be well cared for by Anya's former roommate Amaya, and Mark's condo was finally on the market; leaving all his belongings safely in storage. "Keep this place safe for us Oscar, you're the man of the house!" Mark joked, stepping outside the apartment as Anya made her way back up to double check on him.

Anya heard the little comment he made and couldn't help but snort a little. Mark always seemed to have a way of making her smile or laugh. She was very curious to see how the rest of his family was. Did they have the same sort of humor? If so, she was in for a fun weekend. As long as no one asked her to go swimming. Mark might be okay with her scarred back, but she wasn't really sure she wanted to explain them to strangers. That would not be fun.

"What's with the sour look, babe?" Mark cocked his head to the side after ensuring the door was locked.

"Huh? Oh..." she glanced up at the bright blue sky. It was warm and perfect weather to go to the river. "I just hope no one asks me to go swimming...I mean...I could wear a big shirt..." It was no use in even hiding it from Mark, she voiced all her concerns with him. He did the same for her.

Realization hit him. Her scars. "Don't let that stop you from enjoying yourself, Anya." Grabbing her hand he kissed her palm and smiled his reassuring grin that told her everything would be great this weekend. "Come on, let's go."

Anya was still a little nervous. His mom was still not the happiest that Mark was in a new relationship, despite his feelings being vastly different with Anya. She understood though. Mark had only just gotten out of an engagement and was still getting into a life that was different. It wasn't a surprise that she would have mixed feelings about a new woman being in her son's life. The other dilemma was, how would the rest of his family take to her?

"- and I am sure Minnie has already talked a mile a minute about you to everyone she could get to listen to her." Mark laughed as they pulled onto the highway.

Snapping out of her head she only caught half of what he had been talking about. She hardly even realized they had left. "I hope that's a good thing." Anya laughed as well and gazed at the city that was starting to fade into the background. It was the perfect weather to camp and swim.

"We have been camping in this spot since I was a kid. I know you are gonna love it there." Mark interlaced their fingers as he cruised down the road. "You will also get to meet Phil and Evans' ladies, Kim and Angie." He hadn't talked much about his brothers' wives. "Minnie is excited you will be there." Mark ran a hand through Anya's hair as he kept his eyes on the road. His little sister didn't always take to everyone she met. When Diane had given birth to Maria, there had been issues with her cord being around her neck and deprived her of oxygen for a short time, thus resulting in the c-section. She had some delays developmentally, but it never stopped her. She was advanced in nearly all her subjects. Maria was a great kid and lightened up their entire family and her classes at school. And nothing stopped her from voicing her concerns if she didn't like something or someone. She hadn't cared too much for Lori and wasn't very close to her, but because Mark had been with her for 4 years, everything had just seemed natural.

"There are times I wish I had younger siblings," Anya started as she gave a soft, almost sad smile, "One and done for my family." That was probably the biggest reason Anya had always wanted a bigger family. She wanted her children to have each other. A special bond. "My older cousin Tracy had a baby when I was in high school and I took care of him a lot over summer break."

Mark glanced over at her and saw the small twinkle in her eyes she got when she talked about babies. As quickly as he saw it he also took notice of the small darkness that came shortly after. Anya had voiced at a point that she had no clue if she could even carry a child. Mark knew that possibility probably weighed heavily on her. He also wanted a big family like his, but he wouldn't bring it up again. There was no doubt in his mind that if the time came, Anya would be an amazing mother if she was able to be. He also wouldn't bring up the news about Serenity being pregnant with her and Chase's first baby; a boy. Chances are she already knew. "I think this weekend is going to be kick ass!" Mark gave her a playful slap on her thigh before turning up the music to get her pumped.

Anya tossed her arms up and cheered happily before singing along to 'Feasting on the Blood of the Insane' by Six Feet Under. It was about a 3 hour trip, but it went by quickly with the amount of fun they had on the ride. Anya had gotten several videos of the two of them headbanging to their favorite songs. Before she knew it they arrived to the secluded area that Mark's family occupied every year.

The smell of smoke and grilled food soon wafted into Mark's car and he knew they were close. It was no doubt that his uncle, Ted, was already manning the grill with a beer in hand while everyone set up tents and campers. Rounding a hill, they finally came to the Drummond family clearing and honked a little diddy to announce their arrival. Que dogs barking and Maria running full force towards Mark's car, yelling their names.

"MARK'S HERE!!!! ANYA TOO!!!" Maria cheered, not giving him time to get out of the car before she was hugging him through the window. A few others in his family had stopped what they were doing and went to greet and assist with unloading the car. Many of them had not seen Mark since before his accident.

To no surprise many were shocked or trying to be overly helpful. Mark sighed inwardly, not wanting to be treated like he was incapable of doing things. Glancing over to the other side of the car Anya had gotten out and was twirling Maria around in a circle. "Hey there kiddo!" She smiled into the little brunette's curls and set her down. "Are you liking school?" she asked before going to the trunk to open it.

"Mmhmmm!" Maria gave her a million dollar smile before going on and on about her teacher, her best friend, and of course the little boy who always teases her. "He's such a big meanie!" Maria pouted before trying to take some of the smaller items from the car to be helpful.

"Maybe he likes you." Anya whispered, only to get a major 'Ewwww' from Maria saying boys were icky.

"Anya! Anya! You gotta meet everyone!" She jumped to the next subject of pulling Anya into the crowd of Drummonds. "EVERY-ONE! This is ANYA!" She announced.

Mark facepalmed, it hadn't even been 2 minutes and everything was happening too fast. "Hang on, Minnie." Mark picked her up, giving her a bear hug. "Can I introduce my girlfriend to people?" he growled playfully as he tickled her.

"FINEEEE!" Maria huffed, fixing her hair and skipping over to her cousins. She had wanted to do it.

Shaking his head, Mark looked around. Everyone now had stopped what they were doing and were coming up to the excitement that Maria had started. "Drummond family!" He smiled big, "This is my girlfriend, Anya. Please make her feel like one of the family." A little diplomatic, but that was how he showed how serious he was.

Anya suddenly felt like she had a big spot light on her and it made her a little nervous. Mark started to introduce her to several of his family members by name. Several of them started to bombard her with questions about herself. "O-oh, well I am a physical therapist. I actually helped in Mark's recovery." she gave a proud smile.

Having much approval over the amazing turn around he had experienced, things began to simmer down and everyone went back to setting up their respective areas. Anya glanced around at how strategic everyone was placed. "Mark, is there a specific area we should set up our tent?" She looked up at him as he was talking to Phil.

"Ah yes!" Mark grabbed her hand and they walked over to 'his spot' next to his favorite tree. In big letters carved in it that said his name. "I won this spot when we were kids." Mark smirked his cocky grin. In the distance Evan shouted a 'Fuck you, ya cheater!' and they laughed.

"Language!" Diane shouted from the other side of camp, with a slight laugh. She knew that would not be the only thing the kids would hear this weekend once everyone started drinking.

Anya laughed and shook her head as she pulled out the directions to the tent. Anya hadn't gone camping in a long time, so this was very exciting.

~*What could bring a family together more than camping, burgers, campfires, and some of uncle Ted's famous mason jar contents! More in the next chapter~! Hope you guys are enjoying the story so far! *~

Famous Brew

Before long everyone was gathered around a roaring bonfire, drinks in hand, burgers being distributed around the circle. Anya was laughing at a joke that one of Mark's cousins had made about how they used to play in the woods and came back covered in poison oak. The kids had long since made their way to play in the small creek near the camp. Mark snickered before whispering something to his Uncle. That was when the small mason jar began to be passed around.

Mark took a small sip, hissing slightly at the bite of it. He was already buzzed from the few beers he had shared with his brothers. "Here, baby." Mark handed the jar to Anya who was engulfed in a fun conversation with Mark's cousin Bailee about a middle school fade that had been popular many moons ago. Anya took the jar absentmindedly and took a rather large sip and gagged. "DEAR GOD!" Anya smacked her chest before handing it off to Bailee to regain her breath. "What on Earth?!" She turned to Mark with bewilderment in her blue eyes. "You tryin' to kill me?"

Mark, Ted, and Mark's father all burst into a fit of laughter at the women. "Small sips, babe. That is some potent moonshine." Mark rubbed his thumb over her wet lip. "That stuff will fuck you up big time."

Anya stared at him for a long moment, then laughed with him. "Such a jerk!" she playfully pushed at him. She wasn't mad at him in the least.

Mark threaded his hand behind her head and pulled her into a playful kiss. "I just wanna see you let loose a little more." Not that she wasn't, but he really wanted to see her let go and relax. Knowing full well that meeting someone's family could be very intimidating, a little of Ted's magic brew could loosen up even the tightest person.

After several passes of the shine, several more beers, and wine coolers, the entire family had gotten riled up. The sun had started to set, the kids were tuckered out and the adults were beginning to gain their energy. Bailee jumped up with several other of Mark's female cousins and other women.

"LAST ONE IN HAS TO DRINK THE REST OF THE SHINE!" One yelled loudly.

Uncle Ted choked down his beer "Now, hold up there!" He stood, ripping his shirt off and running after his wife, "That has to last, woman!" Everyone knew he was teasing. The man never came to a family function without at least a few jars on hand.

Everyone was making their way to the creek, except Anya. She was heavily buzzed, but that came to an abrupt halt when she saw where everyone was going. "Oh no..." a small whisper came out.

Diane stood on the embankment with several other of the older women who didn't feel like getting wet. A big grin was on her face as she watched everyone having fun, but her smile quickly faded once she glanced back to see who the stragglers were. "Well, aren't you gonna join them?"

Mark looked over at Anya, sensing her panic. "You don't have to, baby." he reassured her in a low voice so anyone else wouldn't hear.

"COME ON YOU TWO!" Bailee squealed just before her brother dunked her under the water.

Anya bit her lip, and pondered for several long moments. "Fuck it." She steeled herself and pulled off her shirt and shorts. Her hair was up, which would leave nothing to be hidden from everyone around her. "Come with me." A small amount of hesitation still quivered in her voice as she held out her hand to Mark.

Nodding, Mark tossed his shirt over his chair and the two ran down to join the rest of the family.

Diane watched, feeling herself struck with confusion when she saw Anya's back as they passed by her. Mark had mentioned about Anya's accident but never in much detail. Only that it had happened. The scars were deep and jagged along her back. It made sense to her now why there had been some hesitation.

"I wonder what happened." Diane's sister asked in a hushed tone, taking notice herself.

"I have no clue..." Diane watched as the two dove into the water after Mark removed his prosthetic. Part of her still panged with sadness when she saw it, but she was so proud of how far he had come.

Thanks to Anya.

Mark splashed Anya and then pulled her into a loving kiss. No one had said anything about her back, or probably hadn't noticed. Most of the family was already intoxicated. "Having fun, baby girl?" Mark wrapped her legs around him, keeping her close.

Anya's smile was wide and her eyes glittered with excitement, "Absolutely!" she kissed him, almost like a thank you. Although, she felt like they were being watched. The two glanced over and saw Mark's mother looking down at them. "D...Did I upset her or something? She is frowning..." Anya looked down at the rushing water between them.

"No...I don't think so..." Mark was still looking up at his mom and mouthed 'What's wrong?' with a shrug of his shoulders to indicate his confusion.

Diane just shook her head, indicating it was nothing.

"Maybe I should just go talk to her...clear the air." Anya met his gaze.

He sighed, "Don't push yourself too much to please my family. She will come around."

"No...No, I should. We haven't had a chance to just sit and talk one on one." Anya separated herself from Mark, "I love you." she smiled before giving him a quick peck and made her way to the sandbank.

A few of the kids had deposited towels for everyone. Anya grabbed her favorite flamingo towel and made her way up to Diane.

"Having fun?" Diane asked as Anya came straight up to her.

Anya smiled and nodded, "I haven't had this much fun in a long time." She looked back at everyone still hooting and hollering. "But ...I would actually really love to talk with you a bit." she gave a small smile to show she meant nothing hostile by the request.

The other women who were around shifted their way closer to the shore to give the two some privacy. Anya grabbed two chairs and faced them towards the creek. The two women sat down and embraced a small silence between them...well other than the family being loud. "I know things have been very stressful the past few months," Anya started, "and the relationship with Mark and I was very...controversial."

Diane gave her a slight glance and then returned it to the creek, wanting to give Anya time to say her piece.

"I love Mark." Anya said without hesitation. "What that woman did to him...what happened to him afterwards. It was something he never deserved." Anya turned her body to face Diane. "I will never hurt your son. I swear it. Mark is damn good man, he has never once made me question anything about him."

A smile and a nod came from Diane, "That's good to hear."

"I'm not asking you to love me right off the bat. I would never expect that, and you have been more than civil and respectful towards me. I really do appreciate it. I just want you to know that I am very serious about your son. I'm not Lori. I adore Mark for all he is, and I accept everything about him." Anya took a breath, "Just as he has accepted me...and my scars." Her hand went up to her shoulder where some scars showed.

"I saw them...and I saw your hesitation." Diane turned to face her, "You don't have to tell me what happened...but now I can see why you two are meant for each other." She didn't even pause before she pulled Anya into an embrace. "I think you are going to be an amazing part of this family." she shook slightly. "Mini adores you, my husband thinks you are amazing...the family has been saying nothing but nice things about you already."

Anya felt herself welling up inside from her words. "T-thank you..." she croaked.

"I'm sorry if I was hard on you at-"

"Do not apologize." Anya interrupted, "Your son was hurt beyond belief. It was only natural that you should have some reservations about a new woman so fast..." Anya looked over at Mark who was wrestling with his brothers in the water, "Especially such a handsome man." Anya giggled.

Diane laughed as well and the two women continued to talk as the sun continued to go down. Anya finally did tell Diane about her accident and where the scars had come from. Even about how she and Mark had met.

It was a wonderful start to their first vacation.

Expedition

As a thank you to all the amazing support I have received recently I thought I would give you guys a little treat <3 Thank you all so much for your continued support, especially in my funk and crazy nursing journey! I love you guys so much!

Enjoy~

~*18+ Warning*~

Later that night...

Mark and Anya tumbled into their small tent with several laughs and giggles escaping them. It was probably close to 1am and everyone had either passed out in chairs or went to bed in small trickles. Mark shushed Anya's fit of uncontrolled giggling and placed his hand over her mouth.

A happy mistake on his part when he noticed the slight spark in her eyes that indicated she was feeling warm and needy. "Hmm? What's with this look?" Mark asked in a fake confused tone. He got a small whimper and pleading eyes in return. Keeping his hand against her mouth, he slowly stroked his hand up her shirt. She had long since changed from her bathing suit into a comfortable worn band shirt of his that was deemed her favorite along with a pair of gym shorts. Mark felt himself getting hard, and he knew there was no denying the look she was giving him, but they needed to be very quiet so no one heard them.

Chances were though...they weren't the only ones playing the quiet game that night.

Anya couldn't wait any longer. Perhaps it was how smooth things had been, or the fact that she was still slightly buzzed on the goofy juice, the only thing she knew at that point was how bad she needed Mark inside her. As he stroked her skin she worked at pulling off her shirt and undoing her bra.

"Slow down, baby girl." Mark chidded as he pushed her back onto the soft sleeping mat they had purchased. "Don't wanna have the whole camp knowing how needy and horny you are." He purred in her ear. God he loved doing this to her. She loved him in control. Lowering his head he began to lick at her already tight nipples, he knew it would send shockwaves through her.

Tiny wimpers sounded from behind his hand and his thoughts were correct. Her breasts were very sensitive to his touch. Her hands couldn't decide where they wanted to be. Anya went from gripping the blankets to the pillow to being threaded in his hair to pull him closer to her. Every stroke of his tongue on her breasts sent a gush of heat straight to her core. Mark continued to torture her for she didn't know how long, but she was nearly sobbing and writithing beneath him. Begging him to fuck her.

"Do you want me to fuck you?" Mark growled in her ear. Already knowing the answer, he removed his hand for a brief moment to hear her say it.

"Y-yes...please. I need you so bad right now." She tried to whisper, her blue eyes glassy with lust. It was very dark in the tent but the soft glow from the final embers of the fire let in just enough that Mark could see her. He didn't dare turn on their lanturn and give away exactly what they were doing behind the thin walls of their tent.

Mark yanked down her shorts to take not that she was not wearing panties. "Mmm, what's this...? No panties?" Mark sunk a finger into her damp heat as he replaced his hand against her mouth to stop any cries of pleasure. "Soaking wet too." he clicked his tongue and slid his finger deep inside. Anya's hips buckled and she tossed her head to the side, needing that edge. Mark already had her so close. "Such a dirty little thing." He whispered to her and cocked his head to the side. "Turn over." He instructed.

Anya made haste and turned onto her hands and knees, ready for him. She knew better than to make a sound. Just because they were camping, Mark would have still found a way to punish her. Whether it was denying her an orgasm that night or when they got back. A small part of her always sent a small apology to her parents. If they knew how much she loved being dominated by this man, they would probably be in early graves. She had no idea that after their first time together, she would come to discover this side of herself that had been dormant for...well...ever.

She lowered her cheek to his pillow, inhaling his masculine scent, waving her hips at him. Just to be a little more enticing, Anya glanced back at him. "Please?"

Oh how Mark wanted to spank her perfect little bottom, but he didn't want anyone to hear that. This position had taken him a long time to work her up to enjoying because of her scars. Mark loved this position and how hard he could take her. "Not a peep, or else I won't let you cum." Mark whispered in her ear, stroking her clit with small circles.

Anya nodded in acknowledgment, gripping the pillow.

"Good girl." Mark licked his fingers and then gently stroked himself through his shorts. "Now just be a little patient." He stated. Anya knew that meant he was removing his prosthetic again. Despite this being his favorite position it was difficult with his amputation. Mark was careful to position himself just the right way so he wasn't resting on it in a way that would cause pain. "Touch yourself for me, baby."

Slipping her finger from the pillow down to her apex, Anya continued to watch Mark as she began to finger herself. Mark really enjoyed watching her follow his instructions as he worked on his bionic part. Once ready, he positioned himself behind her. "Nice and wet for me?" He questioned, as if he didn't already know.

"Y-yes. Hurry...I feel like I am going to burst..." She pleaded softly as she removed her hand, hoping he would quickly replace it with something much larger.

Maybe it wasn't quick, but Anya got exactly what she wanted. Just painfully slow. "Why hurry?" Mark shushed, "We have allll night." He was teasing, of course. He was way too tired to draw this out for too long. He had bigger plans for tomorrow's expedition.

"Mmmm, noo...faster." Her pleads were soft, and only loud enough for him to hear, she didn't want to have him keep edging her like that.

"No fun." Mark fake sighed and then picked up the pace, pushing them both closer and closer. "Just keep quiet and I will fullfill your request." Threading his hand through her hair he pulled her up towards him, his other gripping her hip hard.

Anya gasped only slightly.

This was new.

And she loved it.

It took everything in her not to scream in pleasure that knocked over her like a tsunami, soaking Mark's cock that was thrusting deep into her at an incredible angle. The sensation pushed Mark over the edge and he came hard, groaning into the crook of her neck. "Fuck yes..." he growled.

Panting, Mark pulled away and discarded his rubber into a bag they had set up for trash. Anya hadn't noticed he even put one on, but he had been very careful lately. Letting out a soft sigh, Anya curled up on her side of the mat and waited for him to join her. She was so satiated and fuzzy, she fell asleep almost instantly as soon as Mark wrapped his arms around her. He followed suit just as quickly.

Waterfalls

Anya was pulled from her dreamy slumber by the smell of bacon and pancakes wafting through the thin layer of their tent. Stretching like a lazy cat, Anya wrapped her arms around her warm partner, waking him in the process. "Fooood..." she grumbled happily.

Mark lifted her tiny hand to his mouth and nibbled softly, eyes still closed. "Mmm I think I like the taste of the lower half." Mark turned and pushed Anya onto her back. Hovering above her, he gave a sexy smirk before kissing her softly.

"Uag you are so predictable with your innuendos." Anya rolled her eyes and wiggled out from underneath him.

"You know you love it." He remarked with a playful slap on her bare ass. Anya huffed and they both proceeded to dress quickly before joining his family around the already roaring breakfast fire. It seemed as if many were still struggling to make their way out of their respective tents after a long night of drinking and merriment. Mark was surprised they were both awake after their fun as well.

Uncle Ted held up a spatula, "Mornin' you two, sleep well?" Mark had mentioned to Anya that Ted refused to let anyone else do the cooking while he still walked this Earth. Both nodded sheepishly before taking two seats near him. "Hungry?"

Mark grabbed himself and Anya both hot mugs of fresh coffee, "I could eat a horse." Mark nodded and took a sip. Anya had grabbed a few bags of coffee from Serenity's shop a few days before they left as a gift to Mark's family. It really was some of the best he had ever had.

"Same!" Anya grinned happily as she nursed her coffee. It was a miracle she didn't have a hangover after the amount she had drank the night before. It wasn't everyday she did something like that.

"You sure can hold your liquor, little lady." Ted gave a belly laugh before handing them both two huge plates of food. Anya blinked in surprise, a little unsure if she could really eat that much. "Eat up you two. Today is the family hike." He held up his spatula and then proceeded to whip up more for others who were making their way around the fire.

A small sigh escaped Mark, and caught Anya's attention. "Are you worried about the hike?" Anya asked him before starting her breakfast. Dear Lord that was good, restaurant quality food. It was a surprise that he didn't do this for a living.

"Can't hide anything from you can I?" Mark gave a crooked smile before continuing, "Yea I am a bit nervous. I'm not going to go the whole distance. I have somewhere special I plan on showing you that is about halfway." He didn't want to let on too much, but it was a place he frequented every time the family gathered for a trip. It was even more special that he never even took Lori to the spot. Anya would be the first.

Giving him her perfect smile, Anya grabbed his hand, "One step at a time. If you need to turn back or take a break we will. It will be nice!"

Anya was right. As always. Mark took in a deep breath as he adjusted the small backpack he wore. It had been about an hour and they were both able to keep up with the family. Mark forewarned his brothers that he would be splitting off to go to his 'secret spot'. Even after all the years that had passed, Evan and Phil still had no clue where his 'secret spot' was. "It's just up this way a little more." Mark held her hand as they continued off a different path.

The sound of rushing water began to fill Anya's ears as they got closer. "Is that...a waterfall?" A gasp of amazement escaped her as she rushed ahead to see the small waterfall roaring over the small cliff. "Mark this is beautiful!"

Watching the ground to avoid missing a step on the rocking pathway, Mar followed her. "I found this spot when I was 6." He wrapped his arms around her from behind and kissed the top of her head. "I had gotten lost because my head was in the clouds." He chuckled. "Luckily after my parents found me I memorized how to find it from the main path. Came here every year after." Grabbing her hand once more, Mark led her off another path that went up closer to the waterfall. "The real surprise is back here. I have never brought anyone else here before. Not even Lori."

Anya was touched by his words. Something she was the first to experience with him. "Mark this is amazing...thank you for bringing me here." Her hand squeezed his a little tighter as she fought not to start crying. Especially when they came up to the small cave behind the waterfall. It was the perfect little getaway.

Mark led her to the middle where he started to unpack his backpack. He brought a sleeping bag and several blankets to make a soft pad on the grass. Next he took out a few small snacks for them to enjoy along with a small bottle of wine. "I wanted this to be special." Mark lowered himself to the ground and pat the spot beside him. Anya was still starstruck before she sat down.

"You really never brought Lori here...but you were together for over 4 years." Anya hated to bring it up, but she was surprised.

Nodding Mark poured wine into their camping mugs. "She hated these trips, and getting her to go hiking was like pulling teeth. We just stuck with the group or she didn't come." Mark kissed her, "No more talking about her."

That was a good idea. Anya rested her head on Mark's shoulder as they embraced the nature surrounding them. They made small talk and sipped wine, occasionally taking a nibble or two of cheese and fruit. One thing eventually led to another and Mark began kissing Anya's neck. "There was also another reason I wanted to bring you here." He growled and unbuttoned her shirt.

"You don't say...here I thought I was going to be part of one of those crazy serial killer TV shows." Anya joked and arched into his touch on her breasts.

"I debated." He shot back at her with a playful snap. At least out here, under a roaring waterfall, no one would hear her screaming in pleasure. He had no intention of holding back like he had the night before. It had always been a dream of his to make love in this spot. Mark was glad he would be sharing that dream with Anya instead of Lori.

"But Mark..." Anya gasped "What if a serial killer hears us having premarital sex! We will be his next victims!!" She over dramatized her acting. "I'm too young to die!"

"I thought I was the crazy serial killer...and since I am...I want to fuck you. Right here." Mark roughly pushed her onto her stomach and tugged at her shorts. "Let me know if this is too uncomfortable. It's grassy but it's still a little hard even with the blankets." He said softly in her ear before snapping off her bra.

Yesssss. This was perfect, Anya felt herself almost purring at his rough, yet careful caresses and nips at her skin. She didn't even notice that the ground was slightly hard. The only hardness she was paying any attention to was the one pressing against her bare bottom. "Oh my Mr. Serial Killer...please don't hurt me. I'll do anything you want." She pouted playfully, continuing to play into the role of the damsel in distress.

Mark had to stop himself from snorting a laugh. She was too much sometimes, but he would play along. That was what he loved about her. "Anything?" He flipped her back over and pulled her onto her knees. She nodded, lust already filling her eyes. Mark embraced her need to try new things. "Suck on my cock, baby girl." he ran a hand through her hair as he freed himself from his shorts. "Maybe I will let you live if you do a good job." He pulled her closer and she responded by sliding the tip of his cock into her wet mouth. The instant he was deep inside a groan left his chest. "Mmm yea...that's it." he guided his dick in and out, gripping her hair. Mark knew she was already wet for him, and enjoying herself. The sweet little sounds she made as she sucked at him told him just that. Mark had never considered himself an exhibitionist, but lately he really wanted to do things he never even dreamed of.

Every stroke of her soft tongue pushed him closer to the edge, "Slow down, baby. We don't need to rush." Mark slipped from between her lips and stroked her cheek. Anya licked lazily at his cock, sending small skitters of pleasure through him. "E-Easy." His breath hissed out.

Anya bit her lip, she had been enjoying that. Mark eased himself down onto the makeshift pad and pulled her onto his lap. It was difficult for him to stand for much longer on the uneven ground. This way was also easier to leave on his prosthetic. Blushing, Anya gazed into his eyes, it was an unusual position for them. Typically Mark kept himself in a position of being in control.

Lifting up her hips, Mark slipped inside with ease and began to thrust his hips into her. The angle hit her in just the right way, causing her to moan loudly. "That's it, don't hide those moans." He instructed, slapping her ass. Another gasp left Anya and she gripped his shoulders as she began to ride him. In this position, Mark had total access to her supple breasts. As she bounced up and down, Mark began to suck and play with her nipples, forcing more moans from her. "Mmm you like that don't you?" Mark teased her nipple.

"Y-Yes!" Anya tossed her head back, her long hair brushing down her back in the ponytail she wore. Mark's hand came down on her ass again, and his name spilled from her lips. His thrusts came into her harder and faster, "Mark! I-I'm cumming!" Anya screamed.

As she came, Mark flipped her onto her back and lifted her hips back onto his cock. "I'm not done with you yet." He growled, pinning her arms above her head with one hand, the other stroked her aching clit as he continued to thrust into her. "I have some new ideas for you once we get home..." Mark purred, slowing his thrusts, "Tying you up...rope...silk...my handcuffs." He licked her neck.

The thought of being bound with his work cuffs sent her overboard. She felt like she could cum again at the idea. "P-please Mark...I want you to do everything." She pleaded. Her lust filled brain could only imagine the things he wanted to try. Things she had only read about in romance novels by Maya Banks.

Mark loved the sound of that, doing whatever he wanted to her. He picked back up his pace and took her harder until she came again. Feeling himself getting close once again, Mark lifted Anya onto her knees and began to stroke himself quickly. Without any instruction Anya looked up at him, rubbing her breasts close to his throbbing cock. While his other hand pushed him towards his climax, the other cupped Anya's face, his thumb dipping into her mouth. "I'm going to cum inside this pretty mouth of yours." He pulled her chin closer and she took him into her once again. Sucking skillfully, Anya pushed him as far as she could take him. Mark finally came.

"The things I am going to do to you when we get home." Mark rumbled low as he removed himself from her mouth. A promise he was sure to keep.

~*Sorry for the delay!! Been a rough couple of weeks...but I hope you guys enjoyed another sexy chapter ;3 Our story is shortly coming to a close. I have a few more fun chapters coming but it's almost a wrap!!!*~

Wanna Go Again?

"OH FUCK! YES! HARDER!" Anya screamed out as Mark took her hard against the kitchen counter. It was clean. Now she would need to re-scrub many parts of the kitchen she just spent the last hour scrubbing. Her cheek rested against the cool marble and she gripped the sides of the counter. She was addicted to him. 2 years together and the fire had not dwindled for either of them. If anything....it burned even hotter.

Mark clenched his teeth, he had regained all his stamina and then some, but his appetite for taking this woman was almost insatiable. "Not yet, baby girl! No cumming yet." Mark held onto her hip tightly, the other threaded through her tangled locks and pulled her head back. He found out she really enjoyed it when he was rough. And Mark...well he loved the look on her face when she screamed out his name when he did it. Mark found out a lot of things that she enjoyed that would shock most people.

Her orgasm built hard and fast. "MARK! OH GOD! Please!" she gasped, eyes rolling back. "L-Let me cum!"

Ever since they decided to start trying to have a baby, things had gotten more intense. He wanted her more than ever since she decided she wanted to have his child. He had almost ended up late to work a few times due to being unable to keep his hands to himself. Sex had never been like this. Ever. Not even with his ex.

And that sex was vanilla compared to what he shared with Anya.

When they had gone house hunting, the only thing on Mark's mind had been, where would be fun places to fuck her. Of course for her, it had been all the important things like the school district and room for a baby. That didn't mean he wasn't thinking of them as well, but it didn't stop him from teasing her when they looked at different houses.

The best part of the entire experience was, despite the hesitation his mother first had when Mark introduced her as his girlfriend officially, Diane grew to adore Anya. She even invited Anya to go out with her and Maria from time to time. Something she never did when Mark was with Lori. Maria, of course, loved Anya from the very first moment, and was still nagging about being the flower girl for their wedding. During the Labor Day weekend together, Anya met Mark's entire extended family. Many of which were shocked to see another woman that was not Lori. Pleasantly shocked. Everyone seemed to really like her. The last thing she wanted was his family to hate her.

Or worse...prefer the ex.

A couple months ago, Anya decided she really wanted to start a family. Mark was over the moon when she had told him she was ready to start trying. He also felt bad for her on some level, because the feel of taking her without protection was unlike any other feeling. The thought of taking her hard and fully, sent the caveman portion of his brain into overdrive. Hearing her needy cries to cum, Mark finally gave in "Cum for my baby...yess that's it!" He shifted his him to hit her in just the right way to send her to the moon and him right along with her.

Panting, Mark held her hips, still feeling the deep satisfaction of her screaming his name. "Marry me." he said, kissing her moist cheek. He had her drooling from their excursion.

Check and mate.

"W-what?" Anya was still dizzy from the intensity he just unleashed on her. She rubbed her mouth with her sleeve. Something about that time felt very different. Was this question why?

"You heard me." Mark chuckled, separating from her. He placed his hands on the edge of the counter to keep himself close to her as she turned. "Ever since you told me you wanted a baby...Hell even before that...I have been wanting to ask you."

Anya felt herself blushing under his intense gaze. That hadn't changed either. He still made butterflies erupt in her stomach and especially after they made love she still felt shy and embarrassed. Mostly because she never expects herself to act the way she does when they do it. Like a sex starved nympho.

"Well...are you just gonna keep staring at me? Yes or no, woman?" Mark squished her cheeks with his thumb and forefinger, smiling his goofy smile.

"I want your damn child ya goof. What the Hell do you think?" Anya shot back at him with a smile and stuck out her tongue.

Mark rolled his eyes and opened a kitchen drawer beside them. "Well how am I supposed to know? Maybe you were just sperm jacking me. Genetic goldmine right here." He teased as he pulled out a small velvet box. A dark part of him almost caught him by surprise when he opened that box for the second time. The second proposal he made. The part of him that threatened to tell him this would end up the same. He shot that down immediately. Mark hated that Lori still from time to time clouded him with the shit she pulled. Even 2 years later.

"Well that was the case at first...buuut...I sorta kinda fell for you." Anya sparkled softly at him, becoming more serious as the box opened. Mark still had trouble kneeling so he just stayed close and revealed the ring he had picked out just for her. Part of him felt a little guilty. It was not as massive and expensive as the one he bought for Lori. they had just bought a house together, so finances had been a little harder. He knew Anya well enough that she wouldn't have cared if she had gotten a bubblegum ring. That didn't stop him from wanting to get her something he deemed worthy of her love, but practical enough she could wear it at work without interfering.

Anya's eyes widened a bit, she wasn't expecting him to actually be proposing to her at this moment when he first said it. The ring box creaked open and she saw the glittering solitaire inside. "Mark...wait...you are being serious?"

"What do you mean? Of course I am being serious." Mark stared down at her staring at the ring. He saw the look on her face. She was fairly shocked. "Why the look?" He smiled.

"I just...I never thought..." she nibbled her thumb nail. "I never thought I would ever be asked. Like...in general. I'm sorry I am just a little surprised you were being serious."

"Well I wouldn't have asked if I weren't serious. I love you, Anya. Marry me." He repeated. Mark knew where her mind had gone, so he didn't need to dig into the comment, just give her a moment to process.

"Oh Mark...you should already know the answer." she hugged him, tears flooding her eyes.

Mark felt relief wash over him, a small part was worried she would say no. "Just don't leave me if I lose my other leg." He didn't mean for that to slip out, and he bit his tongue the moment it did.

Anya gave him a glare. "Don't even joke about that shit." She still waited for the day she ran into that woman and ripped her a new one. But that would never happen. Lori was in New York.

"Sorry." Mark rubbed his neck before going to slip the ring on Anya's finger. "I really didn't mean to say that...I know you wouldn't." He was grateful, the ring fit perfectly on her small hand. "Perfect." he whispered.

Letting out a breath she stared at it, "Beyond perfect...it's beautiful, Mark..." After her accident, she never thought this day would come, where a man actually loved her enough to look past her scars and want to make her his wife. To take her to new heights everytime they made love, just to watch her face as she cried out his name. To want to share a life together, to have a baby. Her emotions bubbled up strong and she broke down in a fit of blubbering tears.

Mark was taken back at the sudden breakdown, "Anya?! W-what's the matter?"

"N-Noth- hic -nothing." She whimpered, trying to smile and laugh while she cried. "I just...you..." sniffle, "I'm so happy!" Anya flung her arms around him and nearly toppled them both over as she hugged him tightly. In her babbling and sniffling, she told him all that was going through her head and how she felt.

The woman never ceased to make him smile. He adored her. "I love you." He kissed the top of her head and held her close to him.

"I love you, too." She sniffled again.

There was a long silence, Mark just held her. "Round two?" he whispered, feeling himself becoming stiff again. How was that even possible?

~Two more chapters to go!!! They will be posted today (I had the story finished, but I wanted to add more meat to the middle)~

Holding Your Breath

8 weeks later...

"Alright Anya! The moment of truth!" The ultrasound tech, Kyle, hummed as he placed the probe over her lower abdomen. Anya worked with his wife, Tracy, who was a nurse on the rehab floor.

Mark's knee bounced up and down as he held Anya's hand tightly. This was the moment he had dreamt of for a long time. In the same notion...Mark was terrified. Anya had already had a rough start to this pregnancy with a lot of morning sickness and migraines. In the two years they had been together, he never once recalled a day where she had ever called off work. Until 2 weeks ago. A trip to the ER, an IV bag of fluids, and a late period. The perfect combination to take a test. A big fat positive. Mark was thankful the fluids had helped, but now he worried about the future and if it would continue. But right now, his biggest fear was not seeing anything on the ultrasound.

"Hmm..." Kyle's brows knit together as he paused on her abdomen, eyes glued to the screen, mouth in a thin line.

Anya felt her heart break. That wasn't good.

Mark's hand tightened on her's and his leg stopped bouncing.

There was a very long silence.

"Well then...that explains a lot."

Anya blinked and jerked her head towards the screen, scared and hopeful. "What is it?!"

"Hold still." Kyle lectured as he moved back into the spot he had been. "Ah, there." He turned the screen to better face them both. "So over here is the gestational sac...and that flicker...the heartbeat." He drew a circle around it, his eyes softened. But a huge smile remained on his lips.

Anya felt herself almost explode with excitement when she saw the flickering of her and Mark's baby.

"And if I shift this..." Kyle continued as he moved to a deeper angle.

Mark and Anya blinked in confusion.

"There is baby number 2." The second image showed two little flickers on the screen.

"Wait...what?" Mark stood, nearly falling on top of Anya in the process so he could get a good hard look at the ultrasound screen. "Hold on...that is 2 heart beats!"

Kyle took a picture and printed it. "Yup, congrats. They're twins. Based on their size you are roughly 8 weeks." He smiled. "But, that would really explain the crazy vomiting." Kyle went on to explain they were called dichorionic diamniotic twins, or fraternal. With a smile Kyle handed Mark the print before heading out of the room. "You get dressed and the doc will be in shortly."

"Mark?" Anya questioned, almost hesitantly. Twins were a huge shock. Anya had a hard time preparing herself to carry one, in the fears her body would not be able to. Even after her OBGYN said she would be perfectly fine to carry a baby.

A soft smile spread across his lips. "Wow...we are having two babies..." Just when he didn't think he could be even more overjoyed. "Anya?" he looked down at her. "Are you okay, babe?"

Anya sat up, trying to process everything when he handed her the photo. Baby A and Baby B marked each of the tiny embryos. "They are so tiny..." she whispered. "Mark...I'm scared..." she admitted.

He frowned a bit, "About what?"

"I know they cleared me...but...I'm just so terrified that...I'm not going to be a good mother. Anything could happen..." Anya teared up. She felt so vulnerable and nervous about everything all of a sudden.

Mark pulled her to him, "Hey hey...no...none of that." He shushed her and gently rocked her. "You are going to be an amazing mother." Mark helped her sit up on the table and wrapped his arm around her shoulder as they stared down at the ultrasound. "You are already great with Minnie, and remember my cousin's baby, Raiylnn? She stuck to you like glue for the whole Christmas party and the cookout a few months ago."

Anya wiped a tear that threatened to fall. "Y-yea..." She let out a breath and smiled. "Sorry...I think my hormones are getting the best of me."

"Don't be sorry about that, baby." Mark kissed her temple. "After we see the doctor, we will get you something good to eat." On que, her stomach growled.

Anya made a sour face at the thought of food, "If I can keep it down..."

Mark felt bad for the doctor who saw Anya, they bombarded him with question after question. Most of which, Anya already knew. She was still having some anxiety about finding out it was twins. As they exited the room, Anya made a B-line for the bathroom, giving Mark a moment to ask the doctor one last question.

"Hey doc...one last thing I wanted to ask." Mark whispered to the doc, making sure the bathroom was shut.

The doctor raised a bushy white brow, almost knowing what was coming, "You can still have sex." he said with a twinkle in his eye.

Mark cursed softly under his breath, the man had read his mind, "Yea but...well...I tend to be...a little on the rough side. Is that going to hurt them?" He half knew the answer, but he needed to make sure. Especially not having any medical training except basic CPR.

The older man paused for a moment, a little unsure of how to respond to the honesty. "Yea...don't be doing anything too rough. No crazy contortionist moves or pressure on the abdomen. Just to be on the safe side." shaking his head as he left.

'That's gonna to be hard.' Mark thought to himself.

Mark watched as Anya ate her lunch. She had a wonderful glow about her now that her nervousness about being a mother had started to subside. "So I think it's time to tell everyone about the babies." Mark said finally, glancing down at the ultrasound photo. He couldn't put it away.

Anya glanced up from her plate. When she did get to eat she tended to shovel it in. Right now she was starving. "I agree. I've been thinking about it since I took that test at home." She smiled happily. ""Twins" means double. I need to reevaluate how to make it fun to tell everyone." Anya wanted it to be a big celebration. This would be the first grandchildren for both their families. Phil and his wife traveled a lot for work and Evan and his wife didn't really want children.

Continuing to watch her, Mark suddenly had the urge to take her home and make love to her before they did anything else. He hadn't had much chance to be romantic with her because of her morning sickness lasting throughout the day. "How are you feeling?" He asked, leaning forward and giving her a look that told her exactly what he felt.

Blush creeped up her face to her cheeks, "B-better, actually, really.. .really good." Just his eyes on her made her hot or maybe it was partly her hormones. She wanted him too. "I'm ready to go."

Mark smirked and leaned back, "I was hoping you would say that."

Mark carried Anya inside, her legs wrapped around his waist and his tongue meshing with hers.

"Oh Mark, hurry." she whimpered, "I feel like I am going to burst."

A deep growl left him, as much as he wanted to take her hard and fast, he would restrain himself. The last thing Mark wanted was to possibly do something to hurt her or their children. "Patiences, my love." Mark whispered as he made his way to the bedroom where he set her back on her feet. "Strip for me, baby." Mark instructed before sitting on the edge of the bed, pulling his shirt off. Grabbing the remote, Mark turned on the radio. He wanted her to strip to some heavy metal.

This was always fun for Anya to do, when he told her what he wanted from her. She liked him in control. Although she wasn't really wearing the right clothes for a strip tease, she made do. Once in her bra and mix matched panties, she began to do a little twirl for him, moving to the beat of the song. Mark was already hard as a rock when she began to give him a lap dance. Mark's hands eased their way up her legs and over her hips and butt as she moved.

"So sexy." Mark groaned as she dipped her butt to tease his clothed cock. Holding her in place on his lap, Mark kissed her neck. His hand moved to cup her breast and the other began to rub her sensitive nub through her drenched panties. "I should have guessed you would be soaked before we even got started."

Anya gasped as he worked at her, completely interrupting her strip tease for him. He is one to talk about patience. Sometimes the man was more impatient than a kid waiting to open their Christmas presents. "Mark...that feels good." she shifted on his lap, trying to ease herself closer to orgasm.

Mark's hand slid under her bra and teased her nipples. "Time to get rid of these." he said through his kisses on her neck. Snapping off her bra, he threw it across the room. If only her panties could do the same thing. "Take them off." he played with the hem of the interfering garment. "Slowly."

Stepping away, she kept her back to him as she slid down the lacy bits of nothing. This gave him the perfect view of her butt. Anya heard him growl. He wanted her bad. As she turned to face him he had pulled his cock from the strain in his pants, but remained semi clothed. He didn't even need to speak the words. The look in his eyes was enough to tell her to straddle him.

Placing her legs on either side of him she eased her way down onto Mark. A needy moan escaped her. Anya began to move up and down slowly. Mark kissed her softly with gentle, steady strokes of his tongue. They didn't make love like this very often, but right now it felt perfect.

The build up of their passion was slowly rising. "Mark...harder." Anya whimpered quietly, trying to roll her hips against him. She needed release. "Please..." her voice cracked.

"No. Not yet." Mark panted. He wanted nothing more than for this to last as long as possible. Continuing to push her towards the breaking point, he kept his pace steady and easy. When she finally came, her body shook and her nails dug into his shoulders. No loud screams this time, but the squeaking whimpers that filled his ears made him fill her with his hot cum. Any noise she made sent pleasure straight to his balls. "Mmm yes...that's it baby." he still thrust, keeping her from leaving the heights she was at. He always said that to her when she came, it made her turn to mush every time.

"M-Mark..." she gasped as he continued. The gentleness he presented was new, but it was powerful and raw. It held the same intensity and passion as their typical sex, just slower and softer. A part of her knew he had done it like this in fear of hurting her. They only did this on rare, special occasions.

He kept her just like that for longer than she could count, thrusting softly into her until he could no longer remain hard.

Resting his head in the curve of her neck, Mark took several deep breaths. "God woman...you...are so fucking amazing." He said with every ounce of pride he could lace his words with. She had given him everything he ever wanted. "Thank you." he whispered, placing a hand on her growing womb.

Anya sucked in a breath and placed her hand on top of his, "We did this." It was going to be a long journey, but she was happy to do it with Mark.

Ghost of the Past, Life of the Future

S everal months later...

Mark glanced down at his phone at the many photos that were being posted on facebook while he waited outside of a cafe. Anya insisted on stopping to pee for what seemed like the hundredth time that day, but he also knew she would be coming out with something sweet. She was 36 weeks and all belly. The twins were growing more every day. They had just had their baby shower and Anya felt like going on a walk before tackling the chore of putting everything away in the nursery.

Mark smiled softly and a picture someone had snapped of them in a moment they thought they had alone. Hands on her belly and a soft kiss he placed on her forehead. In addition to having a shower, they had revealed that they were having both a boy and girl. The first couple months Anya still suffered strong bouts of morning sickness, but as time went on it got better.

Chuckling he continued to scroll through. Everyone had been creative with the gifts; some things a little more eccentric than others.

He loved the glow on his wife's face. Part of him felt a little guilty for not giving her a big wedding, but she had insisted on a tiny ceremony with their immediate families. A backyard wedding, as she called it. Mark always wanted to give her the big moon, but her being the way she was, a tiny model was perfect in her eyes. He had to remind himself she was not Lori and didn't expect extravagance. Even though she deserved it. They had tied the knot when she was showing, and the flowy beach style dress she had picked just made her look ethereal.

Every night they laid in bed he would place his hands on her rounding belly and feel the little kicks. Kicks that told him his children were thriving and coming soon. It was surreal, but he did have moments of panic. A new chapter in his life was coming in just a couple weeks. If she went full term. Twins made that less likely. Anya already had a c-section scheduled. That scared Mark more than anything.

A chill ran up Mark's spine as he waited. Something felt very off, almost insidiously.

"Mark?" A husky voice called out behind him.

Fuck. Mark felt the world shift and move slowly as he turned. Fuck. Fuck. Fuck. Fuck. A million fucks. NO. Mark felt his blood boiling with each nanosecond that passed as he turned to face the woman who crushed him nearly 3 years ago.

"It is you." Lori said, with almost a sigh of relief. She glanced down at his prosthetic, but quickly went back to looking at him in the eyes. "I never thought I would find you again." There was something in her voice...regret? It was shaking a bit.

No words came from Mark, he just stared at her. Slowly he lowered his phone to slip it in his pocket, teeth gritting. What the fuck was going on here. Every idea he had ever run though his head if he ever saw her again disappeared in a split second. He opened his mouth, no words came out.

"I...I am back in Chicago. For good." She started, shifting her purse. Her hair was styled slightly different than it had been. It was in a reverse bob cut with bangs. Still sported the same business attire and stiletto heels. "I had gone to New York and...well I had my first big case as a partner. Politician hit someone with his car and caused a man to lose his leg." She swallowed. "I lost the case, the man got a huge sum...I have never lost a case." A step closer to Mark. "The politician was very powerful and it caused a lot of issues. I was fired."

Mark clenched his fist, his jaw working. Why the fuck was she telling him all this? Why the fuck should he care? He was a little smug about the case she had. Karma. "Why should I fucking care?" he finally ground out.

Lori's eyes teared up. "I made a huge mistake the day I left you. After I got to New York...I couldn't stop thinking about you." she continued to close the space between them. Lori was rambling. She never did that when they were together. "Our passion...our life." She glanced down, "I said horrible things to you."

Mark folded his arms over his chest, unsure of where this conversation was going. Why apologize after 3 years?

"When I got back, I went to the condo, hoping to fix this. But you sold it so quickly. And well...I'm not surprised you blocked me on everything."

"What the fuck is the point of all this, Lori. What do you want?" Mark said annoyed.

"I love you Mark!" Lori nearly shouted. "Please forgive me..."

Mark growled very low in his chest. He had never wanted to hit a woman so badly before. "Forgive you?" he chuckled in a low, very scary way then smiled. "You love me? Where were you when I went septic and nearly died? When I was going through rehab to learn how to walk again? Where the fuck were you when I was depressed in a hospital bed because my fiance of 4 fucking years left me because of an accident I couldn't have prevented. AN ACCIDENT FROM DOING MY FUCKING JOB! A JOB I CANNOT DO ANY-MORE!" Mark yelled. People slowed down to see the commotion. "I'm just half a man!" he mocked.

Lori was stunned. Almost looked...ashamed. Even in the 4 years they had been together, Mark had never screamed at her.

Just then a soft hand touched Mark's shoulder. Anya had just come out of the cafe when she saw him talking to a beautiful woman. When she heard the name, it sent her into a white hot rage. But that was quickly replaced by the most intense pain she had ever felt, followed by a gush between her legs. She had just peed too. Uh oh.

Mark blinked and glanced down at his tiny wife. His tiny wife with a very large belly. "Anya? Are you okay?" He was concerned immediately with the scared look on her face. She had gone completely white.

Lori's gaze shifted to Anya. Then down to her pregnant stomach, catching a glimpse of the matching wedding bands they both sported. Anger snapped in her brown eyes. "Who is she?" Lori questioned, as if she needed to ask.

It took everything in Mark not to completely snap on the woman. Instead he ignored her. "Sweetheart?" Mark rested his hand on her belly and another on her cheek. She felt clammy.

"My water just broke." she whispered with a slight whimper. Mark felt her stomach tighten under his light touch. Her knees buckled slightly.

Mark's eyes widened and so did his smile. He should be panicking at this moment, she was in pain. "You're going into labor?"

She nodded. Glancing at Lori. She had been ready to go after this woman. Guess her kids were non confrontational. The contraction subsided and Anya wiped her tearing eyes. "Hi. I'm Anya Drummound. Mark's wife." She emphasized with a sweet smile, trying to pretend she didn't hear the entire thing. "My water just broke. Our twins are impatient like their daddy." she glanced up at Mark, proudly. "We should hurry. The car is already packed."

"Twins...and a wife." Lori ground.

"Yes. My wife." Mark took Anya by the hand and began to lead her away. "The woman who picked me up after losing a leg and made me whole after a heartless harpy left me." he said as if Lori were someone else.

The two walked together down the sidewalk without a second glance at that bitch.

Once at the hospital, despite her water breaking, Anya still ended up having a c-section. Mark remained by her side the entire time. The twins were small, but their cries showed just how strong they were. Mark held each of his babies while the doctors continued to close up Anya's incision.

"Welcome to the world...Alice...Jett...". Rock 'n' Roll names for his future metal heads. Mark felt at peace holding his children. He took turns holding each with Anya, who was also just as at peace.

"You completed me." Mark whispered, kissing her forehead. "And these two...I overflow." he smiled.

CPSIA information can be obtained
at www.ICGtesting.com
Printed in the USA
LVHW081530141222
735204LV00013B/612